After several years of publishing other people's books, Laurence James decided that it was time he started writing some of his own. So, since early in 1972 he has been a full-time freelance author and journalist.

He has had science fiction short st[illegible] lished both in Britain an[illegible] but the *Simon R*[illegible] in this f[illegible]

His likes [illegible] Braddock [illegible] rock 'n' ro[illegible] dislikes suit[illegible]gs.

Mr James is m[illegible]ried and lives with his wife and three young children in an east Hertfordshire village.

Simon Rack

Earth Lies Sleeping

LAURENCE JAMES

SPHERE BOOKS LIMITED
30/32 Gray's Inn Road, London WC1X 8JL

First published in Great Britain by Sphere Books Ltd 1974

TRADE
MARK

Set in Times Roman

Printed in Great Britain by
Hazell Watson & Viney Ltd
Aylesbury, Bucks

ISBN 0 7221 4979 4

This is for Terry Harknett -
a good friend and a very good writer

Prologue
A View To A Death

'God's wounds, my lord. The dogs run through the brush like scared coneys.'

'Aye, Sergeant. Then let us see if we cannot ride us them down and secure us a fine coney skin or two.'

In the undergrowth four people trembled and panted as they listened for movement from their pursuers. They were all clad alike, in rags that draped over their thin frames and caught and snatched at the thorns. Their faces were pale and pinched, eyes haunted and mouths gaping to pull in the air to their straining lungs.

Eyes met in mute despair as they felt the ground quiver from the hooves of the pursuing horsemen. 'Keep low; by God's grace they may pass us by and tire of their sport. Soft!'

All round the covert where the peasants lay, a band of horsemen stamped and turned, seeking their quarry. Gradually the shouting and the beating hooves faded away, and silence eased back into the forest.

'Father, they've gone. We're safe. Come, Mother, don't weep. This time they've lost us.'

'Aye, Thomas, but we've lost our home. We must now run with the wolfsheads, live in the wild woods, dig for roots.'

'What of that, Mother? Our life is little different under Baron Mescarl. At least we would be free.'

Several minutes passed in silence, broken only by the wailing of the wind and the thin cry of a lone curlew. Then the centre of the briar thicket began to shake and rustle.

Gradually the rustling spread outwards until only a final barrier contained it.

Slowly, carefully, cautiously, four people crept out from the bushes. A man, stooped and shrunken, looking nearly sixty. A woman of much the same appearance and apparent age followed him, painfully crawling on hands and knees. Then came two boys, both ragged and filthy, one in his mid-teens and the other, two or three years younger. Glancing round the clearing, they gradually moved away from their sanctuary towards the dark shadows of the main forest.

They had got about halfway when there was the shrill plaint of a hunting-horn, and the cry of a man's voice. 'Haloo, my lord. The quarry is up!' The cry was taken up by other voices and harness jingled brightly in the cold air as horses burst out of the forest in front of the family.

The eldest son turned frantically, only to find his retreat blocked by a group of grinning horsemen, clad in the distinctive chain mail of the lord's men, his colours blazoned at chest and shield.

Confidently, the ring of men closed in on their prey. The father stood there silent, shoulders dropped in submission. The mother fell to her knees and wept silently, her thin shoulders shaking with the force of her despair. She clasped her hands to her chest in an attitude of prayer. The young boy stood between his parents, hardly understanding what was going on, yet hating and fearing the men who hunted them. Only the elder boy showed any sign of resistance. Fumbling in his belt, he tugged out an old knife.

'Look out, Mathieu! The young boar has one tusk left.'

'Watch out, man! He'll rend you from collar to groin with that fearsome weapon!'

Crying deep in his throat, a low moan with no words, a shriek of despair, young Thomas launched himself at the sneering figure of the noble who led the hunting party.

Laughing delightedly at the unexpected sport, Henri Cherneval de Poictiers tugged at the jagged bit of his black stallion, making the beast rear and thresh at the air with his iron hooves. One fore-leg struck the leaping boy in the chest, hurling him to the soft floor of the forest. There was a sickly crack as he fell, and when he got up, his right arm hung at a useless angle from his shoulder. The men-at-arms encouraged him to fight on, as they would have done at a cock-fight or a bear-bait. Ignoring them, the boy bent down and picked up the knife awkwardly in his left hand and shuffled in, more cautiously.

His father moved as though to check him, but he brushed him aside. 'No, father. At least I will choose the manner of my dying.'

De Poictiers threw back his head at this and laughed. A full, deep laugh, baying from the smoke of his dark beard. 'Well said, young pup. By Mary's womb, if I had not to slay you, I would be minded to take you for the service, though you be full old.'

'Whoreson mongrel! I would sooner die an eternity of deaths than serve you. We know you, de Poictiers, we of the brushwood. We see you fawn in the filthy straw for your vile master Mescarl. I tell you, this is only one ending.' Slowly he came closer to the noble. 'My death is as certain as the rising of the sun. Today it is. But, my lord, your day cannot be far. Even now!!'

As he screamed the last word he dived upwards and forwards, nearly catching de Poictiers by surprise. But his foot slipped on a rotting stump of wood, buried in the leaf-mould, and he lost the vital yard of attack. His knife missed the man's throat and ripped down into the neck of the horse, making it cry out, high and thin, like a wounded girl.

His rider's spurs rowelled him savagely, bringing him back under control. Even while he was doing this, de Poictiers had reached for the ornamental pommel of his sword. The thin steel whispered from its scabbard and lay poised in his hand. Thomas gathered himself for another attack, the knife held outstretched in his good hand.

It was so fast that the eye could scarcely follow it. A hiss of death, and Thomas gazed stupidly at the stump of his left arm, while the blood jetted up and away, falling in silent splashes on the brown earth. The men-at-arms gazed at the sheer speed of it, while the mother closed her eyes and fell back in a faint.

'Fare thee well, dog.' The words were quiet but final. Thomas gazed up at his death and his eyes grew tired. The sword slashed down once more. There was a short, heavy thump on the ground, then a softer, heavier, slower fall.

'Should I kill the old man, my lord?'

'Aye. He knows full well the reason for his death. My lord Mescarl values his deer too well for any peasant to creep around his preserves poaching them. Hang him, and the woman. Mathieu, slap her face and bring her around to this world, that she might have a last look at it before she quits it for ever. Then, hang them together. From yonder oak.'

Three of the soldiers dismounted to carry out de Poictiers' instructions. De Poictiers himself rode his horse in close to the young boy and delicately laid the reeking blade of his sword on the lad's shoulders, the edge leaving a snail's trail of blood on his pale neck. 'Stand still, pup, and you may yet live. Run and you are as dead as your brave brother there.' He moved the stallion so that he was between the boy and the preparations for the hanging. 'There's no need for you to watch that,' he said with what almost came close to a rough kindness.

The young boy looked up at the noble and his eyes were as clear as hill-side pools fed by falling water. For the first time, and the last, he spoke that day: 'Thank you, my good lord. I would watch all, that I may remember all.'

And he stood aside from Mescarl's men and gazed unspeaking on his parents' deaths. The hemp rope went first round the neck of his father, the coarse knot chafing below the right ear. A few turns of whipcord round the wrists, then he was hoisted up on the back of one of the horses, while the end of the rope was knotted round the oak.

'Any prayers, old man? No?' De Poictiers nodded and one of his men thwacked the horse on the rump with his heavy gauntlet. It skittered forward and the body slid inelegantly off its back. There was not even enough weight in the man to break the neck and he thrashed and gurgled, stick legs running in the air until there was no more air to keep the heart pumping and his brain ceased to function. His eyes were half-closed, looking almost disinterested, and his tongue thrust from his mouth, blue and swollen.

The soldiers' efforts to revive the woman had been successful and she came round just in time to witness the final moments of her husband. From the ground she looked up at the arrogant lord, immeasurably high above her; her fear had left her and she had become calm. 'A boon, I would ask a boon. That I may die now and that my boy shall not die.'

De Poictiers laughed. 'Never was a boon more easily granted. See, woman, the rope waits only for your scrawny neck and your brat will become a great man under Baron Mescarl. Why, he may even join the service. Now, away with her. And, you, Simon, swing on her legs to speed her passing. I would not hear that song twice in a day.'

She died more easily than had her man. While she sat astride the great war-horse, her torn dress pulled up over her thighs, she had a strange dignity and the men were quiet where they had thought to be bawdy. Just before the gauntlet dropped to edge her to infinity, she twisted her head back to where her youngest son stood silently watching. 'Remember this. Whatever thralldom may await you, never let them touch your mind.'

As her body fell from the horse, the fattest of the men-at-arms, Simon, grabbed her round the legs and swung his feet off the ground. His weight added to her's snapped her thin neck like a dry twig.

'Shall we cut them down, my lord?'

'No. Let them swing for a few days as a warning to others who would take the Baron's deer. Mathieu, take up the boy and watch him well.'

Suddenly, the quiet forest began to tremble and shake to the echo of a mighty thunder. The horses neighed and reared, but their riders were ready for it. The trees bent to the passing, not far overhead, of a mighty silver and flame creation.

De Poictiers looked down at his heavy chronometer and shouted to his sergeant above the shrinking din: 'The "Zarathustra's" late. Let's hope she carries a good load of pheronium. Remember the last full shuttle? Wine and wenches for three days. Come, lads, make haste for home!'

Formed up behind their leader, the squadron of men cantered off through the wood, laughing and jesting together as men always will after a good day's hunting. Bouncing uncomfortably on the saddle-bow of the soldier called Mathieu was the young boy. He had only looked back once, and his eyes were dry.

After the men had gone, and the sound of their going lingered no more on the wind, the forest crept back to life again. A squirrel chattered crossly at a daw that threatened his territory. A hare limped trembling across the ploughed leaf mould. Moved by a light wind, the two ropes creaked and stretched. The bodies danced gently, bumping and rocking each other. A cluster of bluebottles showed where the man had fouled himself as all his muscles relaxed in death.

A crow perched elegantly on the head of the woman, his shiny black head cocked inquisitively on one side as he regarded the dead face. Deciding all was well, he hopped crookedly on to one shoulder and began to peck out the eyes.

One
A Duly Authorised Organisation

'And in all my born days in the Galactic Security Service I have never stumbled across, even in that sewer of a backworld, Golot Four, never have I seen such crass, such massively stupid, such thoughtless arrogance, such blatant disregard for even the barest essentials, such a lack of care of the minimal requirements, and God knows you two are experts in producing the bare minimum, such a dreck-like attitude. Why, even the rawest grav would have made a better effort. And, Rack, wipe that idiotic grin off your face. Why . . .'

'Oh, great, Bogie! But when he does the "wipe the smile" bit, that's when he rips the top three buttons open on his number ones. And he digs his finger nails into the palms of his hands. Apart from that, perfect.'

'You shouldn't have interrupted me, Simon. I was just getting ready for the foaming at the mouth routine. I swallowed all me spit and I could have choked. Jesus, he's really keeping us waiting this time! What do you reckon?'

'With Stacey, you never know. A lot depends on whether the family of that "trader" complain to the Federation about what you did to him. If they did, then it might be a bit hard.'

'Trader my ass! He was a runner and we all knew it. What he was doing to that lovely little girl doesn't bear thinking on. I just gave him a tiny taste of the same.'

'Ensign Bogart! How can you just sit there waiting for the most serious accusation we've ever faced and calmly say you gave him "a tiny taste of the same". They had to pick him up with a shovel.'

'Worth it though, wasn't it, Simon? Just to see that girl's face when he died. What did you call her?'

At that moment the door hissed open and a stony-faced Senior Security Commander strode out. 'On caps! No talking! Colonel Stacey is now ready to see you. Quick march!'

As they stamped in together, with that minutely exaggerated efficiency that can be recognised as insubordination but not punished as such, Simon Rack whispered the answer to Bogart's last question. 'I said that she was like a golden butterfly floating in an opal mist.'

'Silence!!' The S.S.C. nearly ruptured himself at Simon's flagrant breach of rules. 'Halt! Off caps! Sir,' snapping a crisp salute at the grey-haired officer seated behind the plasti-glass desk, 'Commander Simon Kennedy Rack, 2987555, and Senior Ensign Eugene Bogart, 2895775, reporting as ordered. Sir!' He snapped off another crashing salute and stamped his boots together making the air quiver.

Colonel Stacey raised his head wearily from his papers and waved a gloved hand at the S.S.C. 'All right; thank you, Commander. I don't think we need detain you any further. I'm sure you have, well, things to do.'

'But, sir, are you quite . . . ?'

'Perhaps all that stamping around has made you a trifle hard of hearing, Commander. I said "I don't think we need detain you any further." In simple language that means "out". Now!! And, Commander.' The man turned at the doorway. 'Please don't try and slam my door.'

The door closed so softly that both Rack and Bogart craned their necks to try and see whether it was acutally shut or not.

'Gentlemen.' Stacey's voice was now deceptively soft, but they knew from experience how cutting that soft voice could become. 'Please sit down.'

'I beg your pardon, sir. Did you say, "sit down"?'

The Colonel showed signs of irritation. 'Don't tell me you are suffering from deafness as well, Rack?'

Rack and Bogart sat down hastily in two black chairs, placed at equal distances from the desk and either side of it.

Stacey pushed the papers away from him and sat back, fingers absently touching his chin. Then he reached out with his left hand and pressed a button just under the edge of the desk. A small yellow light pulsed briefly on a control panel set into the padded arm of his chair.

'Just making absolutely sure that we aren't going to be overheard, gentlemen. Don't like these sniffers but it is important that what we discuss today is not repeated anywhere at any time. Is that clear?' Both men nodded. The Colonel stared hard at Bogart. 'And, Ensign, that includes any drinkers or dellos that you might happen to find yourself relaxing in. Right. Have you any idea why you're here?'

There was an uneasy pause, then Bogart began to speak. 'Well, sir, we thought it might be something to do with reports about a runner getting wiped on Sturdal. You see, sir, it was this girl and this man and . . .'

Simon interrupted him. 'What Ensign Bogart means, with respect, sir, is that neither of us have the slightest idea why you want us here.'

'Well, what is that tiny cretin blathering about then? Sturdal? Wait a minute, there was a report that I saw the other day.'

Simon gave Bogie the finger sign that meant 'keep your mouth shut' and went on smoothly: 'Whatever that was on Sturdal, I'm sure it wasn't as important as what the Colonel has called us in for.'

To the amazement – and considerable disquiet – of the two security officers, Colonel Stacey smiled. Smiled! It was a bit like meeting a ferocious tiger on a narrow forest path and having it nudge you in the ribs and tell you a doubtful story. Then, horrors; Stacey actually laughed. It was at that moment that Simon knew that their next assignment was not going to be easy. He couldn't remember the last time the Colonel had even smiled, let alone laughed.

'Simon Rack. You have much to recommend you. Let me see. You joined GalSec eleven years ago at the minimum entry age of fourteen. You did well, very well in basic training and you passed high. Eleven years. Yet, you're still only a Commander. If I didn't know you so well, I'd wonder about that slow promotion. Your record is excellent as far as results go. You have a mission percentage of over eighty. Yet, a Commander! I would say that you are wrecking your career by simple insubordination. What would you say?'

Simon thought for a moment. 'I would just say that I wasn't very good at tolerating idiots. And, the higher their positions, the less I can tolerate them.'

'All right. Now, I don't propose to go through your record or that of the miserable ape who seems to accompany you everywhere. I've seen you before me on more charges than any other three officers of the service combined. Rack, and you, Bogart, I will now say something that I will never repeat, and if I find either of you have ever repeated it, I will break both of you. You will end shovelling shit on a Moon looper. I do not care how much you resent authority. I do not care that you are constantly on charges for insubordination. I don't care that you both hate big-ship discipline. I need a couple of blunt instruments every now and then. And, God knows, there are few instruments anywhere that are blunter than you two. Just, as a small favour, I would be greatly obliged if you would make yourselves somewhat less conspicuous with your hatred of discipline. Because,' he paused to let his words sink in, 'I do need you. And I need you now.'

There was an embarrassed silence. Bogart and Simon looked at each other, at the desk, at their finger-nails, anything to avoid looking at Stacey. Finally, it was the Colonel himself who broke the silence. 'Bogart! Will you stop picking your damned nose!'

Using his left hand on his thigh, Simon tapped out a message and got an instant agreement from his number two. If Stacey was going on like this about them, building them up, it meant one thing. This operation was going to be one tough mother!

After two hours of briefing, accompanied by threedee maps and vidpix on the walls of the office, the two men knew just how tough. Simon looked through his notes and lost himself in plans and memories. He looked up when he realised that Stacey had just finished talking and was waiting for him to give an answer to a question. A glance at Bogart produced no help, so he had to ask for a repeat.

'Rack, I sometimes think you've got a pound of smoke between your ears instead of a brain. I asked you for any questions.'

'Yes, sir. Bearing in mind the Federation's rulings on slavery and linking that with the crucial importance of pheronium in warp-drives, I'm afraid I still don't quite see why you don't have the muscle to put in a star-ship.'

This was the area that didn't interest Bogart in the least. He wanted to know where, how, when, how many, what with, but he never gave one sweet damn about why. As Colonel Stacey explained the subtle problems of intergalactic politics his eyes roamed round the room, following a small fly that hummed inaudibly over one corner of the desk, interested in a smear of shugsub.

'Our information is from a guerrilla force of small numbers and less power. Remember that last time the Federation acted on an unsubstantiated report from a team like that? It was eight years ago and they still haven't put all the pieces back together. We can't interfere in internal affairs, unless there is proof, hard proof, Rack, that Federation law is being broken or that the structure of the galaxy is actually being threatened. Now, if, and I say "if", these reports are true, then the situation is potentially apocalyptic. And, I am not a man given to exaggeration. So, you will draw the necessary supplies and proceed with all speed to Sal Three. There you will do all you can to make speedy contact with the leader of the guerrillas. You have his name? Good. Make sure that your half-wit aide there . . . look at him, watching that fly . . . make sure he has a thorough briefing at sublim on Sol Three's social customs. That's a saving for you, Rack. You won't need more than a quick refresher. From now on you're both off normal duties. Dismiss.'

Simon leaped smartly to attention – when he felt it worth it he would be as smart, or a lot smarter, than the next man – followed instants later by Bogart. As he turned from the desk, Bogart's hand flickered out like a sand cobra and plucked the tiny fly out of the air. The Colonel blinked and tried to work out if he'd seen it or not.

Bogart was first through the door and flicked the dead insect delicately at the left nostril of the S.S.C. still standing stolidly to attention outside in the corridor. As with most things thrown by Bogie, it hit its target and the big officer reddened and started to move. The voice of Colonel Stacey through the open door stopped him in his tracks.

'Simon! Simon! Just one moment. That business that the Ensign was burbling about at the start of our interesting conversation. Some fellow getting wiped on Sturdal. You won't hear any more about it. Unless things don't go well on Sol Three. If you take my meaning. Good. Incidentally, one thing about that affair. Whatever it was. My bugs go out into the corridor there and they picked up some of your conversation. The girl involved. What was it you said about her?'

'I said she was like a golden butterfly floating in an opal mist, sir.'

'Very pretty, Commander. Very pretty.'

Simon Rack, Commander in the Galactic Security Service, marched out of the office and the door slid softly to behind him. Colonel Stacey sat again behind his desk and momentarily rested his head in his hands. Then he looked up again and sighed. 'An opal mist. Great God! I hope Baron Mescarl appreciates a well-turned phrase.'

Two
Red Light Safety

The scout-ship set down among the trees as gently as a wasp on a piece of long-dead meat. The rustle of its sub-warp drive lowered and stopped. The wood was still and silent, the birds and animals waiting to see what this alien invader was going to do. They didn't wait for long.

Only seconds passed before a dull silver panel whispered open in the side of the tiny vessel and two men stepped out. One was short and stockily built, 'like an oil-drum on legs', someone had once said. A clerk at the Commissionary, in fact. The one with the wired jaw and crooked shoulder. That one.

The other was taller – so tall that he would find it difficult to pass for an out-worlder – dark-haired and brown-eyed. Though the dark could have been dye and brown could have come from tinted contax. They wore the anonymous two-piece uniform common to all space-travellers everywhere.

They both held colts – the standard issue GalSec hand-weapons. They were properly called parax-guns, but everyone called them colts. Nobody seemed to know why. The button in the butt was depressed as far as it would go, giving a kill setting over a wide range and scan. Simon Rack and Bogart didn't take chances – unless they had to – that's why they were good.

'Kay?'

'I don't see anyone around. Still, that's probably a good thing. Our man'll get in touch with us once we board at the dello.'

While Simon walked fast around the ship, keeping his eyes open for any intruders, Bogart went back inside to break out their equipment and prepare the camouflage unit. He was still inside when Simon called to him. His voice was low but urgent. 'Bogie! Destruct! Double-A!!!'

To GalSec personnel, there was no more urgent rating than the double-A. When it accompanied an order, it meant, in the language of the regs: 'That the said order shall be carried out with the utmost expedition, and that it shall not be queried except in the case of not hearing or failing to fully comprehend the said order. Failure to comply with a double-A, unless subject to these qualifications, shall be punished as for physical mutiny or murder. (For further details and for exceptions to the ruling – see R.293, (a)-(m) and additional ruling under "Addenda".)'

When a team had worked together as long as Bogart and Rack, often on the far edge of the frontier, those regs weren't necessary. Most of the times either of them had used double-A, lives had been at stake. The unique quality possessed by a double-A is that it operates up and down. If the circumstances warrant it, then a one-egg grav can order the Colonel-in-Chief of the whole GalSec to take a certain action, and he must, and will, obey. Of course, *if* that grav should happen to be wrong . . .

Bogart summed it up once in his usual succinct way. 'If you get a double-A and you're on the can, then you don't hang around to wipe your ass. A clean ass ain't no use to you when you're snuffed.'

During that brief digression, things had been happening in the clearing. Simon had gone to ground on the edge of the trees, colt ready. In the ship Bogart had dropped everything he had been carrying and followed a rare series of actions. In fact, actions he had never actually done for real before. A button was pressed, a handle could then be turned, first left, then right, and finally a switch could be thrown. Get the sequence wrong at the start and nothing happened. Get it wrong at the end and you went up with the ship.

Bogart left their ship at top speed and crash-rolled across the ground, finishing up alongside Simon with his colt ready.

If you'd been watching that scene, you might have wondered how he knew where Simon was, when he'd been hidden inside the ship. Of course, there's a very simple explanation. He just knew!

'Where? How many?'

Simon pointed out straight in front of them, through the thick screen of trees. 'There. Maybe ten. Maybe twenty. Maybe two. I just heard a horse, then another one, muffled.'

Bogart looked at his commander in amazement. 'Hey, the sublim was right! They really ride horses here!' His face suddenly slipped into the terrifying expression that indicated he was thinking. 'Simon,' he hissed, 'how the hell they know we're here? Old man said no sensors. So how?'

'Maybe luck. Maybe they don't even know we are here. We came in low enough to take the fuzz off a bee's backside. Then again, Stacey could be wrong. How long before she brews?'

Bogart glanced down at his kron. 'Three twenty. Since I heard nothing I used a five set.' He pressed his head to the ground to listen. 'They're getting close, Simon. Couple of minutes away. Sounds like about ten. We move?'

Simon looked round over his shoulder, weighing up the surroundings. A party of horsemen was coming their way from ahead. He could hear nothing from behind – might be a trap but it was the only way to go anyway. His old combat-situation instructor, Under-officer Newman, used to say: 'If you got fifty men with colts in front and fifty-one behind you, then you go forward. Only one thing worse than an outside chance and that's no chance at all.'

The horses were nearer now, coming faster. Simon didn't waste any time on talk now that action was close. He tapped Bogart on the left shoulder and pointed back. They moved together, like two parts of the same animal, fast. The other side of the clearing was thick brush rather than trees and they were able to burrow along the run of a fox or badger until they were well inside. By peering through the dry, twisted stems they could see back to the ship. They waited. Still.

Just on four minutes had gone by since Simon had first heard that stifled whinny. Into the open space came nine horsemen, led by a heavily built man, more richly-caprisoned than the humble men-at-arms. Bogart felt Simon tense alongside him, noted the change in the steady breathing pattern.

With a wave of his arm, the knight sent most of the men out in a wide circle about the ship. They heard his voice giving his orders to the three men remaining by him.

'Simon, inside. You two wait with me.'

From their hiding place the Federation men could just hear the man he had addressed, a great fat man, make some complaint back. The knight laughed, a harsh bark, and threw back his head, the afternoon light glancing off the silver hairs in his beard. 'Come, man! It'll wear off a little of your lard.' A note of impatience entered his voice. 'Quickly, you barrel of blubber. I would know if it be empty.'

Groaning and sighing, the fat man swung down off his chestnut and clambered, with much gasping, inside the scout-ship.

One eye on his kron, Bogart silently held up ten fingers in front of Simon. Each second he pulled one down, until there were none left. Simultaneously, there was a muffled, heavy thump from inside the ship and an agonised scream, quickly cut off, from the man.

'Just like a pig when you cut his throat, eh?' said Bogart, pressing his lips to Simon's ear, but was surprised to see no smile on his face.

In the clearing, horses reared and men shouted, while flames spat out of the open doorway. In moments, the whole ship was an inferno, and bracken near to it was also burning.

'My lord, none can live there,' shouted one of the men-at-arms.

It was so obviously true, and the fire was so obviously spreading, that they had scant choice. Spurring his horse savagely, the noble led his depleted troop at the gallop in the direction of the two fugitives. Bogart began to raise his colt, when Simon held him back. Knowing more of horses, he realised that they would not ride through the brush, but would skirt it. And so it proved.

They still lay quiet as the hoofbeats died away. Only when the flames were licking uncomfortably close to their hiding-place did Simon move. As he stood up, Bogart noticed his cheeks were pale and he still breathed fast. It had been a close turn, but they had seen many closer.

'We had best move, Simon. They will be back. Simon!'

'What? I'm sorry. I was . . .'

'I said we must move. Get to the dello with all speed. That big man'll raise the countryside against us.'

'Yes. Yes, you're right.'

After that Simon said nothing until they had changed their clothes to the dull brown favoured by the local peasants. He insisted that they throw their colts far into the flames so they should be destroyed. Bogart protested and Simon snarled at him. 'Fool. If you had stayed awake during Stacey's talk, you'd have heard colts are banned. All weapons except swords and things of that sort of period. Anyone catches a smell of them and we're snuffed. Just like that. Right?'

Bogart nodded silently. Simon turned away and then looked back. 'Bogart. I'm sorry. There is something I've never even told you. Because I thought, well, I thought I'd never need to. But, soon, when we reach the dello, I'll tell you.'

'Simon, I know you come from Sol Three. I felt you when those men came. You knew them. Didn't you?'

Not looking up, Simon stirred at the leaf-mould with the toe of his boot. 'Yes. Yes, I knew two of them. The fat man who died, old Simon. My namesake. And the noble. I know him best.'

Bogart began to walk away in the direction of where they knew the village to be, embarrassed by Simon's obvious depth of feeling. Over his shoulder he threw what he meant to be a cheery word. 'Perhaps we'll not see him again.' The vehemence in Simon's voice stopped him dead. The voice was cold, barren as the dust of the Moon.

'No, Bogie, old friend. You're very wrong. He and I will meet again. I have a small debt to settle up with the Lord Henri Cherneval de Poictiers, bondsman of Baron Mescarl. A debt that has collected a deal of interest over these fifteen years!'

Any drunken customer of the 'Red Mouse' bordello who wandered into Room Thirty-three, known as 'The Priest's Hole', would have thought he'd caught a couple of heshers at their strange unnatural practices. Which would be an odd find in the busiest brothel in all Standon.

On one of the two truckle beds in the small room, two men sat as close together as possible to each other, their arms round each other. One, the taller and younger, had his lips pressed to the ear of the other man, and was whispering intently to him. The other man hardly moved, his face reflecting little of the surprise he felt, his mouth half-open emitting a low, tuneless hum.

When in an environment where sniffers may be found, that was the approved GalSec method for communication. The humming was an added refinement thought up by Simon Rack.

He and Bogart had made their way safely to the dello, avoiding unusually heavy patrol activity by Mescarl's men. The skinny owner of the Red Mouse, 'Long Liz', had taken them at face value as a couple of travelling quack-salvers, resting for a few days before the frantic activity of the Bartholomew's Fair. She had been a little surprised when they refused her offers of women, 'for the time', but they had paid well for their room. And so they should. The Red Mouse was the cleanest dello in the town. And, since rooming-houses of any sort had vanished nearly a hundred years ago, where else would well-heeled travellers come than to Long Liz?

The taller one, Simeon, was a pleasant lad, old beyond his years – but the life of a quack was likely to age a man fast. Now, the older man, Hebadiah (Bogart always had a taste for the odd pseudonym), that was very different. Long Liz recognised him for what he was. A rogue, a lecher and, probably, a cut-purse. She would have an eye to her linen and watch that none of the girls was tempted by his silver tongue and roguish eye to hand out any free samples. If any were to pleasure Master Hebadiah, it would be the mistress herself.

Secure in their room, her guests plotted.

'Simon, you could have told me all this,' said Bogart with a note of reproach. 'But, it is over now. Long over.'

'No. It has barely begun, Bogie. Now we are safely in our base, we must make contact with our man. The guerrillas' agent, Edric the smith, should soon be aware that we are here. It would be better if he comes to us. A place like this will have its share of Mescarl's spies. The walls are crawling with sniffers.'

'Aye. And the beds with bugs that do more than listen.'

'Come; we can do no more up here. Let's go down to the eating-room and force down some of Maid Elizabeth's excellent gruel. And keep our ears open. Some of Mescarl's serfs must come in here at times.'

'From what our best-beloved Colonel was saying, though I dozed for much of it, it seems to me that slaves is a far better word than serfs. And, as for Long Liz's gruel, I have found it useful for cleaning this pig-sticker we must carry here. From its taste, I suspect she had washed her feet in it. Or worse!'

When they got downstairs, they found the communal eating-room was crowded with a noisy throng, and they had to squeeze in together near the end of one of the rough wooden benches. A bowl of soup and a hunk of wheatmeal bread was banged down in front of them, with a metal spoon bearing every trace of its previous users.

The serving-girl, a slatternly apprentice bawd, pushed her way through the jammed tables, ignoring most of the verbal jibes. One large, bearded fellow attempted to get his hands up under her greasy skirts. Without even a word, she cracked him across the pate with fearsome force. The earthenware jug of gruel smashed, spraying the cursing diners with the lumpy liquid. The recipient of the blow groaned once and then slumped face down on the table. Bits of fat and vegetable stuck in his beard and eyelids. The girl knotted her fingers in his thick hair and tugged him backwards off the bench and let him lie in the filthy rushes that lined the floor.

Putting her foot on his back she screeched out: 'One more here. And one for the midden!'

The eaters yelled their approval, while a huge man, a mute, elbowed his way to the girl, bent down, and lifted up the unconscious drunk from the floor by neck and crotch. Amid cheers, he carried him head-high to the back door and through it into the yard beyond. The room fell silent and waited. They heard heavy footsteps fading over the cobbles.

Bogart turned to his neighbour questioningly, but the man held up his finger for silence. Somewhere out back there was a vast splash. Not like water. More like something weighty being dropped in custard. Which it wasn't. Or manure. Which it was.

After the applause had died down, Simon pressed on with his own meal, gradually drawing the man next to him into a surly conversation. His name was Richard and he was a scribe, attached to Baron Mescarl's household. Yes, he knew Edric the smith, but he wasn't a friend. Not at all. Edric was a dangerous man to know. He had the wrong sort of companions. Dangerous companions. Men who wanted to change things. Upset the Baron. But the Baron's chiefest lieutenant, de Poictiers, would soon have them all sniffed out and mewed up in the keep. Pheronium? Everyone knew where it was mined and that the Baron was one of the most important men in all Sol Three for handling it.

Tricky stuff, pheronium. Not that safe to handle. Why, he remembered when a container had split at the shuttle-port and half the serfs nearby came out in fearful burns and buboes. Most of them had died.

Simon was lucky in his informant. Richard was not happy to talk, but what he had to say was interesting. Some of it, like how pheronium came as a by-product of the fission explosions of the big wars, and how, according to him, it was vital to warp-drives on all star-ships, was boring because it was so well known. Even a travelling quack-salver would know all that and Simon politely asked the scribe whether he would like to tell his mother's mother to go and suck some eggs.

Richard got upset at that. 'Listen, quack. Be rude to

someone like me, who has the lord's ear, and you may find yourself doing a job you don't like, with a collar that fits you more snugly than that fustian rag. And one that chafes more.'

'You contemptible worm! You sneak behind walls and talk to honest men of iron collars! Why don't you call them what they are, you mealy-mouthed bastard? Slave rings!'

The intervention came from a man even bigger than the mute door-keeper. His chest was bare and, like his leather apron, bore the marks of a thousand tiny scars, sparks from a bellowed fire of charcoal. Simon caught Bogart's eye. This had to be the smith. Edric. Their contact with the Sol guerrilla movement.

The scribe half-rose to his feet, showing that unpleasant mixture of cowardice and arrogance that any petty official will demonstrate if he feels threatened. 'That's the sort of comment I would expect from you, smith. You and your friends of the woods. My lord de Poictiers will be interested to hear your tale right soon. When I tell him of your words he will be pleased to offer the hospitality of the castle while you are put to the questions. Nay, strike me if you will. But, think on this as the rack stretches your joints, splits your arms from your shoulders, that when you dance from the gallows in the square, I, Richard the scribe, will be there to laugh at you. Now, out of my way, dog, for I am to my lord.'

The smith had his hand raised to strike the smug-voiced informer when he was stopped by a quiet voice. 'Stay your fist, friend. He speaks the truth.'

'Who are you to tell me to hold?'

'I am the salver. Simeon. This is my assistant, named Hebadiah. Strike this rogue and your death will be sure and the more painful.'

'Beware who you call rogue, lest you share this man's fate. For his death is certain.'

'So it is for all of us, Richard. I regret this, but I see no way out. Fare thee well.'

The thin-bladed stiletto slid from the sheath under Simeon's shirt and parted the fibres of Richard's coat as gently as a maid's first kiss. His flesh resisted no longer and his heart burst inside his chest as the blade sliced its walls open. His mouth opened in a shocked and rather petulant gasp, then he slipped to the floor, pulling down the bench on top of him. Like a fish, hooked through the gills, he kicked and thrashed for a few moments. Then, with a thick choking of blood, he was dead.

The dello exploded in screaming, cursing and fighting. Grunting deep in his throat, the mute clubbed down any wretch who came near him. Simon had made for the staircase the moment the knife was out of the scribe's body. He reached the doubtful security of the first landing and looked back at the mêlée, expecting to see Bogart and the smith close behind him.

Overturned tables had checked them and they were fighting their way through the shambles towards the stairs. Bogart cut and thrust with his blade, as casual as though he were at an exercise with Under-officer Newman. A thin smile hovered round the edges of his mouth and he was whistling tunelessly to himself. Bogart was happy. Men fell before him, clutching at themselves, wherever his knife had flicked across them. He was not interested in killing – not when it wasn't necessary – but many a good man carried a scar to the grave with him after that evening in the Red Mouse.

At his shoulder, defending him from any jackal who tried to pull him down from the rear, was Edric. His fists smashed into men's faces and drove them back. They were close to the bottom of the stair when there was a cry from the backyard. 'The lord's men! It's de Poictiers and a patrol! Run! Run!'

The mute staggered from the doorway, plucking helplessly at a crossbow quarrel protruding from his right shoulder. Pushing him aside, in strode the tall figure of de Poictiers, a bloody sword in his hand and his helm thrown back. Around him, panting like a pack of hunting dogs, were a dozen of his men-at-arms. Holding his blade high, the knight shouted at the top of his voice: 'Hold every man here present, in the name of Baron Mescarl! Any man who moves will die. William, ready a bolt for the first dog who even stirs his feet.'

Simon knew when was the time to fight and when was the time to move softly back into the shadows. There was little he could do to help Bogart and the smith, even had he been alongside them. From the landing, he could only watch and wait. He knew that Bogart would not risk a move, outnumbered as they were, though he could see the ensign's lips moving as he cursed the lack of his beloved colt. For a moment Simon wondered if he had done right in discarding them, but the rules on Sol Three against anything but the simplest of weapons were stronger even than religion. Any man, whatever his views might be on Baron Mescarl, would do everything in his power to kill any person who showed a gun of any kind. No, he had been right.

For Edric the smith the odds mattered nothing. He was trapped by de Poictiers. Ahead of him, with his foot poised ready for its first tread, was a staircase that would take him to safety. So, he leaped forward.

'William! Halt me that hind!'

The still air of the room vibrated to the deep thrum of the powerful bow. The bolt whistled through the air and sank deep into the smith's broad back. The impact threw him forward, face down, on the stairs. While the dello watched, the big man clambered painfully to his feet, breath rasping deep in his chest, and began to climb again.

From where he watched and waited in the shadows on the landing, Simon could see the agony in Edric's eyes, the strength of the man as he dragged his body nearer the top.

'Again, William. Bring him down!'

Even as the bolt hummed across the room, Bogart had turned with a cry of 'Nooooo'. His knife crossed in the air with the quarrel and found its target, a second too late. It sliced open the bowman's throat, spraying all around him with a welter of his life-blood. But, his last shot had been true.

At the very top of the stairs, the smith lunged halfway on to the landing, the second short arrow buried an inch below the first, its dark flights soaked in blood.

In the room below there was chaos again as the men-at-arms smashed their way towards Bogart, who had turned like a raggle-haired wolf, his second knife weaving in front of him. The rest of the people in the dello eating-room had dived to the floor, joining the serving-girls under the oak benches and tables.

'Spread out and take him alive. I'll flog the man who kills him to his bare bones. Spread out. Careful, damn you. Alive!'

For a moment everyone was looking down, and the smith was forgotten. Simon slipped from the dark and pulled him all the way on to the landing. As soon as he rolled him over Simon knew that Edric would shoe no more horses. His eyes were beginning to look inwards, contemplating the great journey he was about to take. His breathing was strained and a strand of bright blood bubbled from the corner of his mouth at each breath. For a moment he checked his dying when he saw Simon's face, and felt his arm holding him.

'You are he?'

Simon nodded. Speech was irrelevant now; what the

smith had to say he would tell, or he would die before he could finish it. There was nothing to be done.

'Pheronium. Not just shipped here. Mescarl . . . Mescarl has a mine on his demesne. Uses freemen as serfs and serfs as . . .' A coughing fit interrupted his whisper. 'Serfs as slaves. They die soon. Get to Morkyn. He leads the frees. Guerrillas. Needs help. He thinks there's a plot with . . . with . . . Mother of Jesus . . . other lords. Find him.'

'Edric. Where can I find this Morkyn?'

In the room below Simon was agonisingly conscious that his closest, his only friend was fighting a lonely battle for freedom. Alone. But, this was more important. De Poictiers had screamed that Bogart should be taken alive. While there was life there was still some hope.

In his arms he felt the life slipping away from the large body of the smith. 'Edric! Where?'

'Hail Mary, full of . . . of grace. Blessed art . . . Ooooh, no, no.' His eyes opened and for a moment there was a vivid intelligence in them. 'He'll find you. My mother used to joke that I'd die in a dello.' There was a sharp, convulsive intake of breath, and the body held by Simon felt strangely lighter. As though something had left it. He gently laid the corpse on the landing and snatched a look over the banisters.

Bogart still weaved a veil of death with his blade, humming quietly, teeth slightly bared. The soldiers were not anxious to die, and they could not use the advantage of their broadswords for fear of killing him. De Poictiers stood to one side of the fracas, watching it with ill-concealed irritation.

Even as Simon looked on, the knight picked up a heavy stool with one hand and flung it at the ducking figure of the ensign. Aimed skilfully, it struck him in the chest and threw him back on the stairs. The weight of the blow made him drop his knife and it was the work of a moment for the nearest soldier to leap in and smash him across the top of his unprotected head with the pommel of his sword. Another, bleeding from a deep cut to the cheek, would have slain him, forgetting all in his desire for revenge, had not de Poictiers cried out again: 'No! On your life, Hugh! Carry him out and bind him securely. I would question this rabble.'

'My lord. My lord.' The quavering voice came from an old man or, rather from an old man's head. For that was all that could be seen of him, as it protruded from under one of the benches like the wrinkled pate of a tortoise, peering suspiciously from its shell.

'Come here, dotard. Now, what did you see?'

'My name is Edgar, gracious lord. My son, whose name is perhaps familiar . . .' De Poictiers stopped his rambling by slapping him hard across the face with his studded gauntlet, leaving a trail of tiny bleeding weals down his cheek. 'You old fool. I care not for you or for your puking son. Answer me this one question now. The rest you shall tell my sergeant at the castle later. Was there another with that one?'

'Another, gracious lord?'

With the greatest of efforts, the knight checked himself from crashing his fist into the old man's face again. 'Yes, Master . . . ?'

'Edgar, gracious . . .'

'Yes. Master Edgar. Think now. Take a little time before you answer me. The man who died up there, Edric the smith, and the stranger who will soon be dead. Was there another with them?'

'Another. Aye, the one who slew your archer was named . . . let me see . . .'

'Hebadiah. A quack-salver,' put in another voice, eager that de Poictiers should leave and not look too closely at any others in the dello.

The knight bowed in the direction of the new voice, then turned back to the trembling Edgar. 'We know that he was a man named Hebadiah and he was a quack.' He held the old, lined face in his metal glove and squeezed. So gently that a day-old chick could have nestled safely there. 'Was he alone?'

'No. No. No, gracious lord, there was another. A man that he followed. His name was Simeon and he was also a pedlar of ointments. He ran upstairs.'

The tall man gazed up into the shadows, following the shaking finger of the old man. Even his keen eyes could not pierce the darkness there. 'Mathieu. Take four men and search this warren from top to bottom. The rest of you, beat this stinking mob out of doors and back to their own stinking huts. Then watch every door and window. This Simeon must not escape. The Baron would meet him. As for this,' letting go of Edgar so suddenly that he dropped to the rushes, 'take him to the castle and chain him up. I will talk with him tomorrow.'

Long before Mathieu and his men had reached the first landing, Simon was not on it. Realising that a search was inevitable, he had instinctively climbed higher. Through the dingy corridors, past closed doors and open rooms. Everyone from the top floors had rushed downstairs at the noise of the fight, and he had most of the dello to himself. He knew it would take time to search thoroughly but, equally, he knew that search would be thorough.

All too soon he was on the topmost floor. Easing open a warped shutter, he peered out at the side alleyway, nearly eighty feet below. Round his waist, he carried a thin but strong rope, enough for that distance, but it would not save him from the swords of the soldiers who were already patrolling the area round the Red Mouse, with rush lights casting a smoky glare about them. He had just decided that it would have to be an ambush on the searchers as they came nearer, when he heard a low voice.

'Master Simeon. Have you an ill that I might be able to salve for you? One that might be the better if it were to be hidden in the blackness for a while?'

The corridor was very dark, but Simon could make out the pale figure of a girl, young by her voice, standing in the doorway of one of the small rooms.

He could not keep a laugh out of his return whisper. 'Aye. For my ill could become worse, unless it be looked to with some haste. I fear others come to try and cure me.'

'Come. I know these other physicians, and they be better as butchers.'

Two floors below, they could hear the tramp of heavy feet, and the crashing of furniture as the search went on. They could also hear the shrill whine of Long Liz, as she asked who would pay for the damage. As Simon tip-toed into the girl's room, he heard the deep voice of de Poictiers – that damnably well-remembered voice – telling her that he would willingly pay her price. If she would, in return, pay his price for harbouring enemies of the Baron Mescarl. Simon heard no more from Long Liz.

The girl took his hand and led him through the blackness of her room. She was close to him, and he realised that she was naked. Even at the height of the danger, he felt the blood stirring in his loins. Putting her head close to him, so that he could smell the clean scent of her long hair, she spoke softly: 'You must lie under the bed. It will be a tight fit for a jack of your build, but you should be able to wriggle in.'

Simon grasped her hand. 'No! Blood of the Cross, girl. They will come in here, and they will see you, and the first thing they will do is tip over your bed to see what sort of a rogue may be hid under it.'

He felt her arm shake as she laughed quietly. 'Master Simeon, if that be your name, which I doubt, if they look under the bed they will surely find you. Think you that your chance would be better if you faced them?' Her hands groped at his belt, brushing lightly across his groin, as though by accident. 'And you without a weapon. Or, would you rather play the eagle and soar from that window, high over their heads? No. It is my bed or nothing. If I cannot find some way to turn their oafish minds from thoughts of a fleeing quack-salver, then I am not half the bawd that men rate me. Now, quickly; I hear them on the floor below.'

Sure enough, spurs jingled on the staircase under them. Simon had weighed up the odds even while the girl was talking to him, and had decided that they were heavily in favour of his being taken by Mescarl's men. Therefore he had nothing to lose by accepting her offer of a dubious sanctuary. Dropping to the dusty floor, he wriggled under the low bed. As soon as he was in place, he felt the springs dig into his back when she leaped into the bed herself. Inches from his nose, the girl's face appeared, upside down, like a pale moon. 'Master Simeon, I beg you not to move. Whatever may happen to pass.' Her voice became more urgent. 'Remember. *Whatever* happens, it will be with my urging and will be under my control. Only if things go wrong may you try and help. But, if that happens, I will call you.'

Simon grinned at where he imagined her eyes might be. 'If we survive this night, maid, I will owe you a debt that I will find difficult to repay. And, as for helping you, I fear that I am likely to be hooked by the arse to your bedsprings if I attempt to leap out like a gallant knight.'

She giggled at that, then withdrew her head with a hiss of warning. It wasn't necessary, for Simon had heard the noise of the searching men-at-arms as they wrecked their way along the floor below them. Then he heard the boots mounting the staircase, and the door was flung back. A rush light, smoking and guttering, threw a weak glow round the room. But Simon could see that he shared the space under the bed with a broken comb and a piece of crimson ribbon. Edging his head round to the left, he could see the spurred boots of one of the soldiers.

'Mathieu! Come here!'

More feet from next door, and the sergeant burst into the room. 'Well, well, well. No fox this. But a fine young vixen. Hold the light still, damn you. Now bawd, have you seen a fleeing felon? A quack-salver?'

Simon felt the bed shift as the girl sat up. 'Why, no, my lord. Do I look in need of a physician?' The soldier gasped and Mathieu croaked, and then cleared his throat before speaking.

'Now, girl, will you not catch cold?'

There was no answer. Simon could almost hear the older man licking his lips. He smiled to himself at the thought of Mathieu's reaction if he were to climb out and reveal himself as Simeon the quack. It had been Mathieu who had carried him from the wood the day his parents were murdered and it had been Mathieu's hard hand that had knocked discipline into him. And had often saved him from a worse punishment at the hands of de Poictiers.

Stacey had warned him that their research had revealed at least two men in the Mescarl castle who had known him well as a boy. One was the fat man, Simon, who had perished so conveniently in the blaze of their ship. The other was Mathieu. De Poictiers had rarely deigned to notice a scruffy brat who spent much of his time rolling in the dust of the bailey with the hounds. Even when he was older, the knight had scarcely spoken to him. No, Mathieu was the gravest danger. And, here he was, his toes a couple of inches from Simon's nose.

'Thomas. You go and look in the other flea-pits on this floor. When you've searched thoroughly come back and wait outside this door. I'm going to question this . . . this bawd. And Thomas, don't come bursting in while I'm busy, will you? Unless you want to be on midden duty for a year.'

With a grunt, the other soldier left, closing the door behind him. Mathieu unhooked his sword belt and threw it to the floor, giving Simon a momentary temptation. It would have removed a prime danger to his mission, but there would still have been no way of leaving the dello.

'Oh, my lord! What are you doing? Suppose someone should come and find us, and me an innocent maid? My lord, what a fearsome weapon you have there. By the Blessed Mary, I fear you might split me from throat to belly if you were to . . .'

Her words were interrupted by a squeak, as the burly sergeant heaved himself on to the bed on top of her. Simon almost yelled out loud as the bed crushed him hard into the floor. But, the worst was yet to come. The springs played a painful tune all across his back as the girl and the soldier sported above him. The girl was good at her trade, and took but little time to bring the sergeant to a juddering climax.

'Aye, wench,' he groaned. 'You have a fair field there.'

'Aye, Sergeant,' she replied. 'And right well did you plough it. I shall be sore for days from the pounding of your great leech.'

Mathieu swung his legs off the bed and started to adjust his clothes. 'As for the wolf we seek, it looks as though he has slipped through our net. My lord will be ill-pleased with this night's work. He thinks the salver and his friend may be spies. Once the little man is put to the question, he will vomit up all he knows. Thomas! Is the floor clear? We had best leave.'

'Sergeant. Could I not question the girl a little?'

Simon heard the sound of a blow, as Mathieu struck the

soldier across the head. 'No! You dog. Think on my words about midden duty. Let's go and break the bad news to de Poictiers. After the death of William, he would have had both men. As for you, whore, you had best hold your tongue on this night's work. Then, perhaps, I might allow you to pleasure me again.'

Although he had only the movement of the bed to guide him. Simon guessed that she had bowed to the sergeant. Her tone was mocking when she replied: 'My lord does me too great an honour.'

'Come.' At the door he turned back. 'What's your name, strumpet, that I may know you again?'

'I am known as Sarah, noble lord. Would you not give me a denier, that I may buy myself a new ribbon?'

The sergeant laughed. 'Nay, madam. Old ribbon is enough for the likes of you. Anyway, I can see a piece of ribbon there, sticking out from under your bed. I'll willingly give you that.' To his horror Simon saw out of the corner of his eye that Mathieu was coming back. Would place his hand on the bed, would lean down and would look under it and would see an old acquaintance. One he had not laid eyes on for over eleven years. He was alongside the bed; his hand was on it.

Simon actually saw the insignia on the chest, the black falcon of Mescarl, a glimpse of grizzled beard, then the head was jerked up.

'It is not fitting that a knight should kneel in front of his lady. Let me get it, that I may kneel in front of you.'

Mathieu straightened up with a stifled groan, and coughed out that rich laugh that Simon had heard so often. Generally when someone or something was suffering. Then the girl was out of bed and squatted down near to his head. He saw white thighs, streaked with stickiness, a cluster of dark hair at the pit of her belly, before she rose, triumphantly holding the tatty length of ribbon in her hand.

'Well done, wench. Now you have my ribbon in your hand, I will leave you. Goodbye, Sarah.'

The door closed, leaving only a crack under it for a trickle of light to glow into the room, while the torch was carried to the stairs. Then, as Mathieu's feet stamped down to where de Poictiers waited impatiently, the light vanished and the room was still and dark.

A soft giggle. 'You may creep from your den, quack-salver. The dogs have gone, and the bear can face the night. Did I not say the fool would be easily gulled by the glimpse of a woman's quinn.'

Feeling less than dignified, and blushing in the dark, Simon crawled out. The girl had got back into bed. 'Mistress Sarah, I must thank you for what you did. For letting him . . . Why? That's what I don't understand. Why?'

Out of the open casement, they could hear the jingling and clattering as de Poictiers took his men away with their prisoners. For a moment, there was silence in the cramped room with its sloping ceiling. Then Sarah answered his question. In a way.

'Sit you down beside me. Don't worry, Simeon. I'll not bite you.' A wickedly-timed pause. 'Unless you wish it. No? You ask me why I helped you from Mescarl's lackeys. Some months ago we had a client here, a pilot off the old "Zarathustra", and he was with Crook'd Helen. He'd had a lot to drink. Mixing beer and gin. He got very maudlin, rambling on. Suddenly, he got up, staggered out of the house here and walked down, near to the river. There's a huge patch of nettles and thistles there – where they empty out the night-pots. He stood there looking at this thicket – some of them were as high as your head – and then he stripped off all his clothes, cod-piece, jerkin and all. I can still see him, pale as a willow-root, his little dingle a'dangle.

Gave a great bellow and leaped in the middle. Brin, the mute on the door, had to throw the poor devil a line to drag him out. He was in a dreadful way. Covered all over with stings and prickles. We put him to bed and the next morning I asked him the same question you have asked me. Why? He looked up at me, thought for a moment, then he said: "Because it seemed to be a good idea at the time." '

Much later that night, after Long Liz had done her rounds – which meant another trip under the bed – Simon asked Sarah for as much information as she could give him about the lay-out of the castle.

There was little help there, for few serfs from Standon had ever visited the inner keep. Not of their own will. And, of those that went in, there were fewer yet that ever came out. Sarah seemed to have decided that Bogart was doomed to die, and her only concern was that Simon should not share the same fate. She hated the Baron's men, as did most folk in Standon, for he was a repressive and cruel lord. Much worse of late, she told Simon.

To avoid involving her any further, Simon assured her that the plight of the cretinous Hebadiah was of no further concern to him. That the next morning would see him on his way to the next village where he hoped to find a new assistant who could keep out of trouble in dellos.

Though it was still dark, he could tell that the girl was not convinced by his story. 'Aye, Simeon. I wonder, master, where you are from and what your name is. Tomorrow, as you wend your way to Brakenham, it may just be that your steps could take you near the castle. And, *if* you happened to want to see if any friend of yours was round about that way, and if you went in before noon while the main courtyard was open to traders and if you slipped away by the furthest door, then that's as far as I could help you, but that would put you into the main body of the castle.'

'That's a deal of ifs, Sarah. Maybe in the morning I will count them and weigh them.'

'And now?'

'Now, I will show you what an ill-trained oaf that sergeant was.'

Three
Parlour Games

Castle Falcon stood on a small rise to the north of Standon, its gaunt battlements dominating the surrounding countryside. A stagnant moat lay around it like a rotting girdle. The only gate into the outer bailey was a wide, studded affair of double oak, with a heavy drawbridge and an iron portcullis within. The courtyard was overlooked by high walls of granite, hewn centuries ago. The black Tower held a museum of forbidden arms, explosives, gas and even fission weapons. Heavily guarded, it was the only such armoury in the Northern Hemisphere of Sol Three.

A far more narrow postern gate opened on to the inner bailey, with the Well Tower, King's Tower, Queen's Tower and Falcon's Tower – overlooking a precipitous drop – all around it. The main banqueting hall lay near to the Queen's Tower, with the kitchens alongside.

The walls were an average of twenty-five feet thick. The garrison, under the command of the Seneschal, Henri de Poictiers, numbered over four hundred men. The castle also held upwards of two hundred serfs, mostly garnered from the village. It was a dark and chill place, wherein was happy none but Richard de Guesclin Lawrence Mescarl, twenty-fourth Baron of the line. A line that stretched back unbroken to the wild days after the end of the neutronic wars.

Mescarl was a middle-aged man, fatter than when young Simon Rack had bowed the knee to serve him rich, sweet wine. He had succeeded to the title at an early age. His father, known locally as 'Black Roland', had been found in his bed after a night's debauchery with a fish-bone stuck in his throat. It was admitted he had choked to death, but questions were asked. Like, why had he such an expression of bloody rage on his face? And were there not several fish-bones, and did they not seem to have been jammed down his gullet? And, how had the late Baron managed to bruise his own throat?

But, as is the way when a noble dies and his son immediately succeeds to his title: A bird that fouls its own nest is considered the height of stupidity. So it was with servants. Roland's eldest son, Robert, succeeded to the title and managed it well. For the twelve days that he lived to enjoy it. The accident that robbed the world of three members of the Mescarl family, Robert, his younger brother Geoffrey, and the elder sister Ruth, was really a most extraordinary affair.

A slight malaise of the digestion had saved Richard from joining them. A fishing expedition on a lake four miles away turned to tragedy. Nobody knows exactly what happened. Simply that the boat turned over some distance from the shore, and only the two boatmen struggled safely from the water. They, poor fellows, having survived one disaster, promptly ran into another. For, in the woods, they encountered young Richard, recovered from his upset stomach. They gasped out their news and were rewarded by being cut down on the spot by the new Baron Mescarl. It was an action typical of the man he was to become and effectively removed the only two witnesses from the earth.

Standon gossip had it that other eyes had see what happened that hot summer afternoon. That they had seen the boatmen club the family and then, and only then, tip the boat over deliberately. The new Baron had changed the family motto from 'Always With Humility' to 'Never Wrong'. And no man had yet come along who could disprove that.

When he heard the news from de Poictiers of the brawl at the Red Mouse and the killing of the smith, it was early morning and he was preparing for a day's hawking. The Baron and his Seneschal were closeted together for twenty minutes and when they came out they were both smiling.

Bogart was thrown into the dungeons and tied, but not chained, to the wall. By then he had recovered consciousness and was treating his captors to a fine flow of abuse on the subject of freedom for travellers and what he proposed to say to this Baron Mescarl who encouraged his louts to murder and plunder innocent men. Though he was a great believer in hope, he had noticed the thickness of the walls and the depth at which he was imprisoned, and his hope was faint.

Although Bogart was unable to hear the din from where he was in the damp and black, the market had begun in the outer bailey. From all the surrounding countryside serfs and freemen brought their produce to the castle to sell and barter. Security in the general demesne was relaxed for the day, though the guards on the Armoury were doubled.

Simon found it easy to get in through the massive gates. Sarah had provided him with a cloak and a basket which he had filled with eggs from an old woman on the road. She was happy to save a day's bartering and accepted his inflated price with ill-concealed glee.

Carrying his provender, he moved slowly through the noisy, sweating throng, deliberately asking too high a price, lest he lose his reason for being there. Under the hood of his cloak his eyes roved around the walls, seeking some way in. For a moment he regretted he didn't have a grav-pack that would have taken him up and over the walls. He also felt naked and unprotected without a colt on his hip. The short sword that swung against his left thigh, and the two smaller knives, one nestling in the small of the back and the other in a soft pouch at the nape of the neck, did little to make him feel any happier.

Sarah had given him enough information to get through into the castle proper. Few had the knowledge that could take him from there to the dungeons, but he knew enough from his life there to remember that the path lay ever down. In all the years he had lived in Castle Falcon, he had never been down that deep, though he felt fairly confident that he would be able to locate them. Then, it was merely a matter of finding his trusty aide and getting out scot-free. A mere matter!

First there was the postern gate. Simon suddenly turned away into the throng and began to offer his eggs at a far lower price. The peasants instantly sniffed the bargain and pressed around him. A loud voice shouted for them to make way and Mathieu pushed him out of the way as de Poictiers swaggered past. The moment the knight and his attendants had gone by, Simon doubled his price and the crowd drifted away, leaving him alone. Simulating a hacking cough, he staggered over near to the gate and collapsed on the ground. In fact, he had no real plan at all, and was just testing reactions and exploring one or two options.

Crawling to the wall, he sat with his back to it, holding his precious eggs close to his chest. One of the guards came over and stood looking down on him. 'What's wrong, friend? Sun a bit much for you? Why don't you come and take a seat inside the gatehouse here with Harold and me?' Letting things move him gently along, Simon clambered to his feet and allowed the guard to take his arm and ease him in to the shade.

Harold was younger, much younger, than the other guard and much less happy about sharing his room with a stinking serf. Simon made haste to try and win him over. 'Pardon me, master. But, would you and your kindly friend here care to have one or two of my eggs as a small token of my appreciation for your great kindness to such a humble person as myself?'

The first guard shook his head and continued to gaze out over the busy market, but Harold was less cautious and took not one, not two, but a dozen eggs from the basket. Then said gruffly, 'I thank you, Master . . .? Master, whatever your name is. I've not seen you here before, have I? I don't even think you're from Standon. Hey, Rolf, d'you know this fellow?'

Rolf turned quickly and came back into the room. 'What?'

'I said, did you . . .?'

'Never mind. I'm sure I spotted that cutpurse over by the silk merchant. That's where de Poictiers was going. Jesus save us if he gets his purse lifted. Come on, Harold.'

'But what about him?' pointing at Simon, who was just beginning to show signs of recovery.

'Blood of the Cross, man. Would you see us both at the whipping-post tomorrow, even ere we break our fasts? You, Master Eggman, stay there till we return.'

As he went past him, Harold gave him a clout across the side of the head with his mailed fist. 'There'll be more of that if you move.'

Then they were gone, out into the bailey. There he was, clutching a basket full, or nearly full, of eggs, with only an unguarded door between him and the inner bailey. Simon thought for a moment on the wisdom of taking the cumbersome basket but decided it had a twofold value. If he left it, then Rolf and Harold would know he had fled and would soon raise the alarm. Also, it might yet provide him with a pass to take him a little further along the road towards Bogie.

He edged the heavy door shut behind him and paused for a couple of seconds, taking in the well-remembered scene. Yes, the Well Tower rising on his left, then the King's

Tower. Straight ahead was the granite bulk of the Falcon's Tower – if Mescarl were in residence, that's where he would be. Unless some poor bastard strayed over the harshly-drawn line and was paying his price in the Torture Chamber for the pleasure of the Duke and his current mistress. Then on the right was the main block. The Queen's Tower. Odd how these self-promoted warlords had stuck to the old titles! On the ground floor of the Queen's Tower was the banqueting hall and, next to it, the kitchens. Simon rubbed his right hand against his shabby cloak, remembering the times without number that he had burned that hand turning a roast of pig on the kitchen spit. How plump Simon had once thought it a famous jest on the young boy from the brushwood to make him ladle the scalding fat with his bare hand. Well, Simon had been well-larded in the burning ship.

'Just who in the name of all the Blessed Saints are you, and what are you doing here in the inner bailey?'

The speaker, who had come out of a low door to Simon's right, was somewhat younger than he was – a skinny woman, her dress marking her down as a middle-order servant, and her red and floury face showing her to be a kitchen attendant.

Simon tugged at his forelock, and attempted a clumsy bow. 'Beg pardon, mistress. Sergeant Harold in the guard-house there . . .' pointing back to the postern, praying that the said Harold might not burst angrily through it at that moment . . . 'he said that I was to leave these eggs with them, but the other man, Rolf, said that it would help that pretty, slim young maiden from the kitchen if I were to bend the rules and regulations a little and take them all the way through for her. They did mention the name of this said attractive wench.'

The lanky hank of a slut actually bridled and blushed. 'Would the name they said be "Charity", think you?'

Simon cudgelled his head as though he would beat out his very brains. 'Charity. Charity? Charity! Now, now. I vow that it were not Faith. Charity?'

The woman danced up and down in impatience. 'Come, come. The name. You must remember it.'

'Anon, anon. 'Twas not Faith and 'twas not Hope. So, I am decided. It *was* Charity.' He stopped and looked the woman straight in the eye, mustered his face muscles to make sure they would not betray him, and asked: 'Why, mistress? Do you know this lovely Lady Charity.'

'Why, fool, did you not recognise me from what they said? I am Mistress Charity. Now, give the basket to me and be off with you.'

As she tugged the eggs one way, Simon pulled them back. 'No, sweet Charity. For if I return this fast, they will know I've disobeyed them. For they commanded me to take them all the way to the kitchen, to save your pretty arms from the strain.'

As he expected, the skeletal slattern simpered and flounced ahead of him towards the kitchen. Simon was glad of her company, for they twice encountered parties of guards, but Charity clove through them with her bony, high-slung breasts, shrugging off any attempt to delay her. Simon scampered along in her wake, like a scout-ship following a star-cruiser through a shower of meteorites.

Finally, they reached the passage-way leading to the castle's vast kitchens. There she insisted on taking the basket from him. Simon feared she would call a guard to escort him back to the outer bailey, so he pressed close to her.

Nearly dropping the basket, Charity slapped him away. 'What do you think you're doing, peasant. Get back to your fields you dung-grubber!'

Simon ran back down the corridor, turning to shout back: 'I only wished to savour one sweet kiss from the lovely Mistress Charity.'

Amazingly, she blushed yet again. 'Fie on you. If I told my husband, Harold, what you just said, you saucy rogue, he'd give you a fine buffet. Away.'

Safely round the corner, he paused to relax his face in the laughter that had been threatening to burst from it for the last five minutes. 'God of all the galaxies, she really had been married to that brutal ox on the postern! What a mating they must have. Either he smothers her, or she shreds him to pieces.'

Recovered and purged by his mirth, Simon went more cautiously on his way. From the kitchens his path led him downwards, through stone alleys and stairs that grew ever narrower. 'Mescarl must be feeling more secure,' he thought; for the corridors were less well-patrolled than when he had lived there. Although Mescarl's special body-guard, a hand-picked and cossetted band of some sixty highly-skilled killers, were reserved for the duties of guarding the Baron and the Armoury, there should be ample of the other troops. Yet, he could hear no footfall. The other thing that he noticed was that the ways were better lit than fifteen years ago.

Down miles of stone paths, past open gates and unlocked grilles, Simon made his way below ground. The air grew steadily more dank and foul, and once something scuttered across his foot, making him jump and curse in the silence. He was into a part of the castle strange to him, and he stepped carefully, measuring each decision at each turning.

Once the passage darkened, and he stepped even more lightly. It was well that he did, for his foot felt the edge of a pit just in time for him to throw himself back and down. His breathing quickly returned to normal, and he went on, leaping the drop. Many would have dropped some pebble or trinket down the abyss, to find the measure of their escape. That Simon did not, was a measure of his unique talent. He had escaped and that was all that mattered to him.

He cared not if the drop were ten feet or a thousand feet. It would all have been one had he dropped into it.

Incidentally, had he dropped a small stone it would have fallen for eleven and a half seconds and would have landed with a barely audible, echoing splash.

As he crept on his way, a tiny vid-scope, set high in the shadows, swivelled restlessly to and fro, like the eyes of a paralysed man.

A blind corner, putting half his face round first, peering. Only a foot away from the frank, open face of a guard, leaning against the wall, helmet down by his feet. Relaxing. Waiting for his shift to end, normally a double shift but something about changing routine to keep on their toes. All he wanted to do was finish and walk out into Standon with a couple of cronies, drain a few jars and, if his savings ran to it, pump some of the dirty water off his chest in either the Red Mouse – blast, that was off limits after William's death last night – it would have to be the Pussy Basket. He smiled at the thought. Then he saw this half of a face appear round the corner from the upper level.

He opened his mouth to give a challenge. Not really a serious one, because it couldn't very well be an enemy. He would have had to pass at least three checks, and he would have heard the noise if there'd been any fighting. So, it must be one of his mates. That was why he moved so slowly, with no feeling of urgency.

Simon, on the other hand, felt a desperate sense of urgency. He slid round the angle of the rough wall, his knife ready clasped in his hand, point upwards. His left hand, fingers stiff, stabbed for the guard's eyes. To protect himself the young man pulled his head back, exposing the neck. Simon lunged with the knife, feeling its needle-point slip up under the man's chin, through the inside of his mouth, crunch through the thin skull and penetrate the brain.

He held the handle firm, against the twitching of the

head as the nervous system tried to cope with this massive and deadly assault. And failed.

Simon had used a knife to kill in that way before, and he noted that this time there was not the familiar feel of stubble against the back of his hand. The boy he had just killed was not even old enough to shave yet.

He tugged the body, bleeding very little, into the darkest of the cross-passages and went on. Another vid-scope circled and peered aimlessly above his head.

This part of the castle was old, older even than the Mescarl dynasty. Older, possibly, than the neutronic wars. This deep, way below the green fields and trees, hewn rock could have survived where a whole world nearly ceased to be. It was possible. The striations on the rocks, walls thicker than the mind could imagine, all spoke of antiquity. Dark, damp, oppressive. Simon came at last to the iron bars that closed off the dungeons. Beyond the bars, old beyond rusting, Simon could see a row of low doors, wooden and heavily-studded with iron. A small grille at eye level and another near the floor. That, and nothing else. No guard. No lock on the gate. A bunch of keys hanging by one of the doors. That was when Simon Rack became certain that someone was helping him. But who, and why? To Simon, those were just irrelevancies. There was only one way to go.

On.

His acute hearing was suddenly aware of a sound. Mumbling up from beyond one of the locked doors. If they were locked!

He walked carefully over the worn steps, stopping at the bottom to listen again. No sound apart from that monotonous humming. A noise approaching a tune, but never quite getting there. Not the first door, or the second, or the third, or the fourth, or the fifth. But, it was the sixth. Coincidentally it was the door outside which hung the bunch of keys. Some old and red with decay. One bright and oiled.

Simon pressed his ear to the cell door. He needed only to catch an odd word to know that he had found Bogart, Ensign. It was a fair wager that there would be nobody else in Castle Falcon who would know all the words of 'Spacer Jane' – an unbelievably long and repetitive ballad covering the various adventures and sexual misadventures of a young, nubile lady Commander of GalSec. Bogie was just coming up to one of the better and more whimsical passages where the heroine enters a body transference warp, which leads to a strange rearrangement of her orifices. The possibilities are nearly endless, and all very, very crude.

'Pssst!'

'Piss off, you dreck-faced hesher!' The song continued.

'Master Hebadiah in case there are ears listening, will you cease? Master Hebadiah!'

'Simeon? What in the name of this dreck-infested heap of straw kept you?'

Simeon was not surprised to find that the bright key was the one that fitted, nor that Bogie was tied with thin cord, and not chained or manacled to the dripping walls. His knife flowed through the bindings, and Bogie was free.

Using the same technique that they had employed on the bed at the Red Mouse – it seemed days ago, but was still a bare half day – Simon filled Bogie quickly in on what had happened and what he planned. He missed out no fact that was important, nor included any that were extraneous. It was of no concern to his friend how he had got there to rescue him. That would be for later over a bowl of mead. It was enough that he was there.

'One last thing. They were on to us much too quickly when we landed. Mescarl's got some sophisticated sensor gear about the place. Also, this whole scene here has been too easy. Only one guard, doors open, keys ready. I've spotted a couple of vid-scopes as well.'

'Vid-scopes! Here in this old heap! I'm surprised they've got any power source to run one.'

'Well, they have. Now, they wouldn't have recognised our ship. It wasn't marked, and the self-destruct would leave nothing for them to work on. So, they probably don't know who we are, or why we're here. We hope. So, let's make a move, and I'll brief you on our second cover story. I fear that Master Simeon and Master Hebadiah have but a short time for this world.'

At that moment, all the lights went out.

There was the faint hiss of compressed air, and then the heavy boom of two weighty metal doors engaging. The echoes had hardly died when the lights flickered once, then came on again at full strength. When Simon and Bogart looked round the cell area, it took bare seconds to notice the changes. The old rusting bars were gone, withdrawn into crevices in the roof. In their place smooth durstel rods, thinner than a man's little finger, yet the strongest metal alloy known to the galaxy, had dropped pneumatically into the gap, forming a tight web. An impenetrable barrier. Bogart walked casually over to them and ran his hand down them, feeling the characteristic oily patina that typified durstel.

'No way.'

'Is that the only way in and out?'

'I've not had any chance to look. No food and a bucket of very cold water. Nobody looked in on me, but there were definitely guards out there. I heard them. Fact, I heard you soft-footing down here. I reckoned if I played dumb, I might just get a break. Then I recognised you from the way you put your feet down. Softer than most. Anyway; no, I don't know of any other way out.'

Simon looked around, then opened each of the other cells – none of them were locked – but there was no way out. While he did that, Bogart wandered around, pausing here and there to tap on the flagstone with the hilt of one of his knives. As Simon repeated the procedure in each of of the tiny cells, Bogart whispered: 'Here. This one's hollow.'

Sure enough, it lacked the infinite deadness of the other stones. By working the blades of their knives carefully into the crevices round the block, they were able to begin edging it up. To their considerable surprise, it came up easily. So easily that Simon chipped at it and found his knife would break bits off. 'I don't get it, Bogie. It's not stone at all. It's some kind of extruded plastic imitation. Only weighs about a third what it should. Now, why would Mescarl put this in the middle of his dungeon? Careful now, it's nearly up. Christ!'

The gasp was for the hideous charnel smell that burst up at them the moment the false stone was lifted. It was the odour of long-dead things, of rotting flesh and of pale creatures that feed on such stuff. It was so nauseous that they nearly dropped the block back again, but just managed to swivel it away on to the floor.

Behind them, deep in a corner, hidden by the shadow of an ornamented cornice, a vid-scope glanced round the dungeon with a strange kind of bored indifference.

The pit beneath the flag was so dark that no light was reflected into it. Simon tried to bounce some of the indirect light with the blade of his knife, but the gleam died in a couple of feet. But, that was enough to show a metal rung on one side, and what looked like another just below it.

'I've seen nicer escape routes,' said Bogart, wrinkling his nose at the miasma that boiled up from the hole.

'At least it's a way out of here, even though it goes down. I didn't know there was any way to a lower level here. What do you think?'

'I don't see much choice. Do you? Listen.'

Somewhere above them they could hear, faintly but

becoming closer, the clash of running feet, mailed boots, even the jangle and crash as someone tripped over a trailing scabbard. Bogart leaped for the hole when Simon grabbed him.

'Wait. Listen!'

'Are you going slappy? Come on. They'll be on us in a moment.'

'Wait! Bloody listen! That knock on the head in the dello must have scrambled what brains you ever had. Don't you notice anything about the noise?'

Bogart stood by the pit and listened. 'No. Apart from the fact that they're getting awfully close. They only sound a couple of floors above us. And one of them's clumsy and keeps on tripping over. . . . Right!! It's loop tape. But why?'

Simon rubbed his finger along his nose. 'They wanted us to rush down that hole. Kneel down and grab hold of my wrists.'

As they got in position, the noise above reached a thunderous crescendo. And stopped.

Wrinkling his nose against the stench, Simon let Bogie lower him gently down until his foot touched the top rung. The moment any of his weight transferred to it, the mortar holding it in place crumbled and it dropped away. Swinging freely in space, Simon listened for a thud or a splash that would tell him it had reached the bottom. But there was not the whisper of noise. Unless, Simon strained his ears, unless there was the faintest of rustlings, immeasurably deep, as though something scaly had been disturbed in its slime. At the same time, there was a fresh wave of the evil smell.

'Lower. I'll try the next one.'

It held, as did the one below it. Using his belt, Simon was able to steady himself as he went down, then help Bogart swing down in his turn. The tunnel dropped vertically, with sides as smooth as wet glass, about one metre square. Above them, as they climbed carefully down, they saw a gleam of light in the dungeon, grow even smaller, until it shrank to a pin-point star.

As they went deeper, the actions became mechanical – right foot down, left foot down, right hand down, left hand down. Until, so suddenly that Simon nearly lost his hand grip, there were no more footholds. For a few moments he swung there, feet scrabbling desperately at the sides of the pit, breath rasping in his throat. He felt, to his horror, the prickling in his right shoulder, beginning to work its way down his arm. He knew from the bitterest experience what would happen when that feeling reached his wrist and hand.

Shaking his head to dash the burst of sweat out of his eyes, he managed to pull himself up on to the rung above, where he rested, panting. Far below him, he heard – or thought he heard – that rustle again. They had got used to the foul stink, so he could not tell if it worsened momentarily.

Drawing a deep breath he hissed up to Bogart, waiting anxiously above: 'That's it. No more steps. I swung down and there's nothing. We'll have to go back. Bogie, on the way up, feel all the way round the sides. There might be some kind of side tunnel.'

The dot of light grew painfully larger as they climbed back, until it seemed like an unwinking eye, regarding their puny efforts with an unmoved interest.

The side-tunnel was there, on the side opposite to the rungs of the ladder. Bogart scrambled in first, followed by Simon. The sides were smooth, but the floor was rough. It began at one metre high and gradually grew higher, until there was enough clearance to stand upright.

The path began to incline upwards – a long and winding path. If they'd had a compass, it might have been possible to keep their bearings, but in that dark it was out of the question. Even Bogart, with his uncanny sense of direction had no idea where they were. Just that they were going upwards, which had to be a good thing. Deep below the earth there were too many things that may have once been alive and maybe still were.

They climbed for over an hour, feeling their way forward carefully in case there were more death traps. They took it in turns to lead and it was Simon who found the door, blocking off the path completely. They each ran their fingers over its surface, seeking a clue to open it.

They agreed it was durstel again, featureless except for a small mesh grille, about four centimetres across, set exactly in the centre.

Bogart probed at it with his knfe, but it didn't yield at all. Simon again ran his fingers over it and then put his lips to Bogart's ear. In the dark he misjudged and found himself whispering into his nostrils, but that was swiftly remedied. 'I reckon it's a sniffer of some kind. It may even be the key. It could be that the right code word will open it up. Equally, after that damned ladder with its trick rungs, the right word might blow us from here to Golot Four.'

Bogie crawled up to the door and put his mouth to the grille. 'Come on magic door. Open. Bloody open!'

It is truly said that many a right word would be spoken in jest. The door was programmed to open when the right word was spoken. The word to open it was, of course, 'Open'.

Both men shielded their eyes against what seemed a lightning bolt of blazing light. In fact, the light was fairly dim, but after the pitch blackness of the tunnel it dazzled the pupils. Once they were accustomed to it, they could see the passage again became lower, shrinking back to its one metre height. The side walls were white, metallic plastic of some sort. Light came from protected panels in the roof. The floor surprisingly, was of rock. There was still a gradual but steady incline.

'No point in hanging around. Let's go.'

Behind them, Simon was aware that the panel had closed again. During this part of their escape, the crawl became slower as the walls came in. What was more worrying was the way panels came down at irregular intervals to shut off any retreat. Not that there was anywhere to go back to.

'Simon. It's getting warmer. In fact, it's getting bloody hot. The walls are heating up fast.'

Not only the walls. A few metres back, the stone floor had given way to the white plastic, like the walls. Most of the heat was coming from the floor. One of the sliding doors had just hissed shut behind them, so there was only one way to go. The burning was worst on the areas touching the floor – the hands and knees.

'Bogie. Rip off your jacket and try and tie strips of the cloth over your hands, and try and keep your knees up. Kind of hop along.'

As soon as they had done that, the travelling became less painful. The climb grew steeper and, for a time, the heat increased. The light cloth darkened and scorched, smoke making breathing less easy. Even the soles of their shoes began to singe.

Bogie turned to face Simon, his face streaked with dirt and running with sweat. 'I reckon this is getting a bit much for me. I feel like a raisin in a piece of stuffed spaghetti. If it gets hotter, you can soak me up in a sponge and carry me out in your back pocket.'

'Hey, I reckon it's getting a bit cooler! Yes, it is. And the passage's widening again. Just in time too. What's left of my jerkin wouldn't wrap up the collected wit of Colonel Stacey.'

They both broke up at the thought, and found themselves able to stand clear upright. In front of them the tunnel forked, one fork continuing upwards, and one plunging back towards the depths of the earth. Simon pointed to the one that went down, and was rewarded by a slightly raised eyebrow from his companion. 'Ever since I got into Castle Falcon things have gone my way. As soon as I got you out, everything's been a cheat and a deceit. The most likely option has been the most dangerous. Therefore, the upwards path seems the most likely so we'll ignore it. Off we go again.'

The two men had hardly entered the tunnel when a door edged slowly shut over the other option. Then, there was a dull thud, as though some large creature had thrown itself against the barrier.

It would be monotonous to recount the next couple of hours, for Bogart and Simon simply trudged along the well-lit corridor, sometimes down, but generally up, until they saw ahead of them a blank wall. Unlike the other doors they'd faced, it seemed integral to the structure. As they got closer, they saw it was a wall and not a door. But, at the bottom of it was a circular black pool.

'What the fugg is that?'

Simon dipped his finger into it, very carefully. 'It's about body temperature. Denser than water. Could be anything. Whatever it is, that's our way out. I'll go first.'

'Pray pardon me, sir. I'm a better swimmer than you. Also, I'm going. Bye.'

Before Simon could move, Bogie had plunged into the dark liquid and vanished. No bubbles broke the surface. Nearly a full minute went by before there was a disturbance in the pool. Simon was so amazed at what came to the surface that he nearly forgot to reach down and tug them out. Instead of Bogart's head, it was his feet! The scorched bottoms of his shoes waved in the air helplessly. When he was once more right way up, he leaned against the wall and panted. His hair was matted to his scalp and his eyes were bleak. 'No chance. This bloody dreck gets denser as you go on. I got under some sort of barrier and then it got thicker and thicker. Like shugsub syrup. We'll have to go back.'

Simon shook his head. 'I don't think we can. Listen. And that's no loop tape.'

Not all that far behind them, slow and patient, they heard again that dreadful rustling of ancient scales scraping on the stone floor. Every now and again, the thing gave a wet, rasping cough, as though it was voiding its gullet of some noisome liquid.

'Master Hebadiah, have you a salve ready to keep us from the Great Worm? No? Then let us tackle this pool.'

The surface of the pool was too thick to carry any splash as the two men dived in. Bogart went first, trailing their two stout belts in his hand behind him. Simon followed immediately. The black fluid washed over them, and then it was as though they had not been. Simon felt the barrier scrape at his spine, then he wriggled under it. At once, he noticed the liquid had become denser. Bogart flailed his feet just in front, unable to generate any purchase and swim upwards to the life-giving air. If, indeed, there was any air above. Simon's last thought had been what a nasty ending if they got through to find that the ceiling the other side came right down to the level of the liquid.

They'd soon know. Simon reached up through the treacle until he held both of Bogart's feet. A quick tug and then he pushed up with all of his strength. At the same time, Bogart kicked back. The resulting energy burst was just enough. Simon felt the feet wrenched free from his grip. Then, nothing.

He hung in the utter dark, feeling it press in on him like a suit of tight black rubber. Seconds flashed past and he felt his lungs stretch as the air was used up. He tried to keep still, not to panic, to conserve the moments of life left to him. When there was no more hope, that would be the time to use up the last dregs of air in a desperate attempt to break free.

Something banged his chin and he grabbed it. It was a foot, with a length of leather tied round it. Sweet Golgotha! Once Bogart was out there was no way he could get the belt back to Simon, except by risking his life by coming back into the pool.

Holding the leather firmly clenched, he again shoved with all his failing strength. The feet disappeared and, almost at once, the strain was taken up on the belt and he was pulled from the clinging embrace of the bizarre syphon. Near the surface on the far side, the fluid was close to being a solid, and he marvelled at Bogart's power that he had been able to struggle out. Even with help, it was all he could do to clamber on to dry stone again.

'By all the wounds, I thought I shouldn't be able to get you through. That stuff is the devil.'

'Better that than the devil we left the other side, Bogie. Though, I have enjoyed a swim more than that one. I swear it took me back to being in my mother's womb. Ugh!'

Bogart was still trying to wipe the sticky mess off his face, but with scant success. It coated both of them from head to foot. 'Simon, it proves what they say about the old books. There is a deal of wisdom in them.'

Simon gave up the struggle to get clean and just wiped his eyes clear. 'What makes you say that?'

'Well, I remember in one of my favourite old stories; someone is always saying: "A black pool opened at my feet, and I dived into it." Just like us!'

Another half hour's walking brought them into a large chamber with a vaulted roof. The floor was sanded and showed signs of being brushed smooth.

'Notice the air? It's lots cooler than it was, and there's a draught. Coming from over there.'

'There' was a pair of doors, chased bronze, with immense hinges. Bogart walked to them and pushed gently against them. The doors were so finely balanced that they immediately started to swing open. Bogie reached for them to try and stop them, but, with impeccable timing, the lights went out again.

Cautiously, back to back, Simon and Bogart edged out through the open doors, shuffling over the sand. They had gone perhaps thirty full paces when a movement of air behind them told of the doors closing. The heavy ringing as they slammed together whirled about like the sounding of a vast gong.

Both men had their swords drawn, facing out into the blackness of what they felt to be a big area, bigger than any chamber they had yet come across.

The only sound they could hear was the rushing of their own blood through the caverns of their skulls. Above them someone clicked their fingers once, and the lights blazed down on them. A soft voice spoke: 'Welcome to my home. My name is Richard de Guesclin Lawrence, twenty-fourth Baron Mescarl. And who, pray, are you?'

Simon shaded his eyes against the light and looked up at his questioner. He saw the Baron, plumper than he remembered, surrounded by ladies of his court, with a smaller number of foppish nobles. As far as he could see de Poictiers was not there. Neither was Mathieu. He and Bogart stood in a large arena, perhaps fifty metres across, with a row of dark cages around one side. The walls were smoothed stone, six metres high. Mescarl and his sycophants hung over the low balcony, fanning at their nostrils with lace kerchiefs or swinging porcelain pomanders.

'Come, my revolting friend. I have asked you your name, and I will not ask you again. I will simply have one of my arbalestiers cut you down. I would regret that on two scores. I do not like killing a man, or even a serf, without first knowing at least his name. Secondly, you and your stout little friend have given I and my friends a deal of pleasure and amusement over the last few hours.'

'You watched us? On your damned peepers.'

'Of course. What other point would there have been in letting you into the castle? You were watched all the way. I may say that no man has ever done one half as well as you two did. Which makes me sad that I must kill you. But wolfsheads such as you only foster discontent. I take it you are from Morkyn's band? No matter. Come, a last time. Your names?'

'Simeon, my lord.'

'Hebadiah, my lord.'

'And you claim to be . . . what?'

'We are travelling chirurgeons, my lord. My assistant here has great skill with the mixing of salves, while I am well-versed in the treatment of disorders of the eye and the cutting out of stones.'

'You lie. Do not interrupt me! Master Hebadiah, what would you prescribe for my Lady Jocasta here, who has a most painful tooth-ache?'

'An ounce of piretre root. Bruise it and crush it and immerse it in some six ounces of spirits of wine. Put a small quantity of this sour red tincture in the mouth and leave it there until, saving your grace, the mouth fills with spittle. . . . I have not known it necessary to repeat this in all the hundreds of cases I have treated.'

Simon breathed again and thanked the skilful scientists and researchers of the sublim branch.

Mescarl was obviously surprised at the facility of Bogart's reply. But his suspicions were not any manner abated. 'And now, Master Simeon. If you have such skill with eyes, how would you prevent the inflammation? Eh?'

'Why, my lord, the answer depends on what kind of inflammation there be. If it be the bleeding, or the itch or the evil humours. But,' he went on hastily, 'if it be a simple swelling and pain, then I would take a pound of both Roman Vitrol, a dangerous substance, my lord, and Bole Armoniack. A pinch of Camfer and pestle them together until they were well blended. I would take a little of the mixture and dissolve it in a litre of boiling water. After stirring, I would let it all settle, then decant what is needed. A few drops before you break your fast and a little before retiring for the night, will cure the worst of eyes.'

There was a silence for the space of twenty heart-beats in the arena. Then Mescarl turned to a man behind him. 'Fetch de Poictiers. He's where? Blast and bloody damnation! What of the old dotard from the dello? Dead! I had said he was to be put to the question. Not slaughtered. I will hear more of this. So there is no case against these filthy creatures? What?'

As Simon and Bogart watched, Mescarl went out of their sight to confer with one of his officers. The nobles continued to watch them with a lively interest, as befitted men who seemed to have leaped the Styx and rejoined the human race by a miracle. One of the ladies ogled Bogart and 'accidentally' dropped her handkerchief near to him. Bogart picked it up with a cheery wave, wiped his nose on it and threw it back to the sand. Then Mescarl reappeared.

'I crave your indulgence for this delay, my friends. No doubt you had thought to be long dead by now. I am told that the main reason for holding you, Master Hebadiah, was that you killed one of my bowmen and attempted to aid a suspected rebel. The witness against you for sedition is sadly not able to help us further. So what say you to the charge that you tried to help a wolfshead?'

Bogart answered: 'My lord, I saw only a man – a person I had never met before that evening in the bawdy house – who was attacked by a stranger, a scribe I believe. There was a fight and the scribe was slain. Then your bullies came charging in, firing off their quarrels in all directions. So I tried to stop a senseless killing. In so trying I fear that I killed one of your murderous crossbowmen; if that is a charge for death, then you must slay me, for I am guilty.'

After a moment's pause, Mescarl clapped his hands slowly. 'A fine speech. You are a warlike leech. Both of you showed more courage below us here than I would have thought possible. Why, my Lady Jocasta became so excited when, when things became warm, that she quite forgot her larks' tongue pie. You did well. Since I would not waste two such men in a killing, I offer you a choice. Enter my service with the ranks of sergeant in my personal bodyguard. What say you?'

Before they had a chance to reply a new voice, deeper and firmer, interrupted. 'Your pardon, lord. Absalom would not return after he had killed. I beg your forgiveness for my tardiness. If it please you, lord, I would ask these men, before they join you, one question. Apart from wondering why they seem to have been sleeping in a mountainous midden. I would ask the taller one this: How came you to this place? And, why did you destroy your ship?'

Simon allowed the hum of comment to subside before he replied. 'I see that nothing can be hidden from any servant of Baron Mescarl. Truly, my lord,. you are right to be suspicious. We are quack-salvers. But, we are more. My friend and I have fled from the oppression on the Earth colony on Mars. We were mercenaries there. We came here to join the guard of Baron Mescarl, for we hear the pay is good and the food better. And that there be exercise for any man who can use his sword and his wits. The fact that we are here at all shows that we are men of some mettle. Since we cannot now join in our own time, unnoticed by keen eyes such as yours, then we would join now. And here.'

He drew his sword and reached as far as he could towards Mescarl. 'My lord, you know now the full truth of who we are and why we are here. We would both pledge our swords to you. To be your liegemen in both life and limb. To lay down our lives unquestioning for you. Will you take us, my lord?'

Mescarl turned across to where de Poictiers stood. 'Take that gruff expression off your face, you old bear. If they be not spies, then they are fine men for our guard. I will recount privily to you the deeds they have done this day. And, my worthy Seneschal, if they be spies, then where better for them to be than in your company, under your eyes from morn till night? Smile, damn you, de Poictiers! See to it.'

Simon and Bogart bowed to the back of the departing Baron and his train of lords and ladies. No sooner had they gone than de Poictiers ordered one of the men-at-arms to throw over a rope ladder. They stood before him above the sandy arena and he recoiled from the stench and oiliness of them.

'First things first. Let us see what you are like under that filth. Go and report to Senior Sergeant Mathieu and tell him to take you both for a bath. Then report back to me. And don't try and put anything over on him. Nothing escapes the falcon's eye of old Mathieu. Right?'

Four
Deliver Us From Evil

Steaming water gushed out of the brass faucets so hard that it took away the breath and reddened the skin. The coarse soap felt gritty to the touch, but removed the stench of the castle's bowels and the black ooze of that noisome pool.

Dirt flowed down their faces from matted hair and whirled over the white tiles and vanished through the circular drains. Water streaming down his body, Simon's thoughts were speeding around the many problems that faced him. Now he was in Castle Falcon, with the dubious distinction of being a member of Mescarl's bodyguard, would he be able to find out anything of the rumoured cabal of nobles on Sol Three, of the threats of slavery and, most important, of the threats to the galaxy's supplies of pheronium – a vital element in the warp-drive of all star-ships?

But he and Bogart had a far more pressing threat – to themselves. Just across the shower-room, invisible through the steam, was Master Sergeant Mathieu Scrimgeour. Probably the only man in the entire castle who might reasonably be expected to recognise in Commander Rack – or, as he was known, Simeon the salver – the young boy who he had helped train for four years, the boy he had seen off to join the Galactic Security Service at the minimum age of fourteen. A boy who had been a bitter weight to discipline, and who had proved unsuitable as a page to de Poictiers. And, most importantly, the man who had helped hang Simon's mother and father for poaching in a barren clearing fifteen years ago.

Now well into middle-age, Mathieu no longer rode out with his lord on errands against the brushwood renegades. His eyes had lost none of their keenness, but a stiffness in the shoulders restricted him chiefly to administrative duties within the castle.

'Ho, in there, that's enough. You'll use a month's water ration if you scrub longer. Come out here and let's see what you're made of under that dirt. Quickly! I'm turning off the water now.'

The hot jets wasted away to a mere trickle, though the steam still hung thickly in the air. Simon drew the naked body of Bogart close to him and whispered urgently in his ear. Bogie nodded and suddenly slumped to the floor moaning.

'Sergeant. My comrade Hebadiah has turned his ankle on a piece of soap. Lend a hand.'

Mathieu walked carefully in through the shower, his boots squishing through the pools of water that lay on the tiles. 'God's blood and hair shirts, what a maladroit fellow he must be. He's better suited to a stable orderly than a sergeant in the bodyguard. Come then, my pair of roosters, come put your arms round my shoulders, carefully, damn you!! Now, let's get you out. Incidentally, don't think yourselves promoted yet. That rests with my lord, the Seneschal, and he's not an easy man to convince of merit.'

Gasping under Bogart's weight, the sergeant slipped and slithered out of the showers until he could lay him gently on a pine bench in the ante-room where they had stripped off their stinking garments – what was left of them.

Pressing his hands on his hips, Mathieu straightened his shoulders with a groan, throwing his head stiffly back. He was still standing like that when Simon struck him. It was a brutal blow, designed to totally incapacitate with great pain, yet not to kill. It was delivered with the hard edge of the right hand, chopping upwards into the soft underbelly, unprotected by any armour in the safety of the castle.

The big man gasped in agony and doubled forward, his hands grabbing at his groin. He retched up his evening meal, splattering the floor, and fell to his knees, head bowed, groaning and mewing to himself.

Simon stepped in, carefully avoiding the vomit, and tugged his head back by the long hair. The face that looked up at him was that of an old man, torn by bewilderment and pain. The eyes saw nothing but a blurred face gazing down at him. His mouth framed the word 'Why?', and Simon, for all his bitterness, could no longer find it in him to hate the man. But he was in too deep and the stakes were far too high for pity to check him.

Bogart was busy at the controls, turning them as high as they would go. Scalding water hissed and bubbled in the pipes, and even the ante-room began to fill with the steam.

'Bogie! Turn it off.'

'But, you said . . .'

'Just bloody turn it off!'

'I thought you wanted to boil him . . . make it look like he had an accident and got scalded to death when he fell.'

'I did, but I don't now. Get a mop and clean up this mess in here.'

Gradually a spark of knowledge was coming back into Mathieu's eyes, and he peered into Simon's face, seeking some clue.

The younger man squatted down beside him, holding his head in his arms. 'A hanging. Many years ago. And a brat who wouldn't cry. Remember, old man?'

The mouth opened, and a whisper crept out. 'Simon. Simon Rack. You've come back to kill me. All this terrible distance just to kill me.' The face was almost proud.

'Yes, Mathieu. Just to kill you. You taught me too well. Too well, Mathieu. You said, never to leave an enemy alive. For one day that enemy would ride out of your past and cut off your future. Remember?'

The greying head nodded.

'I would give you time to make your peace with your Maker, for an old dog like you should have need of it. But I fear it would take more days than I have minutes. So it must be now.'

'Quickly?' The voice so quiet that Simon had to lean forward to hear it. Even as he laid his ear by Mathieu's ear, the sergeant tried one last, desperate gambit. His hands clawed up for Simon's eyes, raking at his face. But he still wore his heavy gauntlets and could not grip. Simon parried him easily enough and held him firmly with both hands under the chin.

'Aye, quickly; you foxy old bastard.'

There was almost the shadow of a smile, as though Mathieu knew the race well-lost, and did not grieve overmuch. Then Simon slammed the head back against the tiled wall with all his strength. Even the thick hair could not cushion against such a fearsome blow, and the bones of the skull smashed with the noise of a ripe apple falling on to stone. The whole body relaxed, and Simon held only the corpse of an old hatred.

Bogart looked down. 'He was a game old devil. Eh? But why did you not make him suffer for his slaughters?'

'He but obeyed his lord, de Poictiers. And, Bogie, I looked down at him, and he is an old man. Much the age my father would have been. There may be truth in the saying that revenge is a dish best eaten cold. I fear that my dish has cooled over-much in the years of waiting. As a boy, I used to take myself to sleep in the straw settle, in the

Well Tower over yonder, imagining how I would one day kill every man in that party. Now they are all dead or scattered. Simon died two days ago. Now Mathieu. There are only the top two left. I would give this oldling as easy a passing as I could. Now let us clean up and call for help. It was the old man's heart. A chest pain, then the thud of his fall. There was nothing more we could do.'

The interview with de Poictiers had been far from pleasant. He had been suspicious of them before the death of Mathieu, and he was now doubly suspicious. Fortunately for them, Mescarl had insisted on sitting in on the interrogation, and was obviously minded to believe them. Boredom was the Baron's greatest enemy, and any new face or new toy was likely to keep his favour. For a time.

So it was that they had left the chamber of de Poictiers with no noticeable stain on them. It was well known in the castle that Mathieu had not been well. The pains that had crippled his shoulders had obviously spread to his chest.

The only unpleasant moment was at the end. De Poictiers had paced the rich carpet in silence, deciding what to do. Finally he had given them a stern, cold warning of what would happen if they once stepped out of line. Or if they were involved in any other mysterious deaths. They had been put instantly on to double duties. The lord had stood directly in front of Simon and gazed into his eyes.

'That means hard work. You understand? Strict discipline. What you went through on the Mars colony is nothing to what you'll go through here. Very well, Master Simeon.' He tapped him on the chest with a thick forefinger. 'And guard that expression on your face! Otherwise the protection of the Baron will not save you from a flogging. Remember, he is a cruel man, who enjoys the suffering of others. At the moment you are something new.

Men who have lived when no other man has survived. But he is fickle. Your novelty will keep you for a few days, a week, no more. Then, you must stand without it and prove your value. As we all must.'

Simon and Bogart turned smartly, clicking the heels of their new boots, shoulder-straps creaking – as new leather will – mail coats chinking softly. 'Corporal Simeon! Have you ever visited Sol Three before? No? Your face has a cast to it that seems familiar. Your mother was not from these parts? No matter. Both of you, if you wish to be sergeants in a few years. Step lightly. Take great care at the banquet tomorrow. There will be many important lords from all over the world. Perhaps the greatest gathering that Castle Falcon has ever seen. Be on your guards. At such times, treachery most often walks hand-in-hand with false friendship. To your quarters now, Masters Grave and Fetter.'

There was but little need for a talk that night for Corporal Simeon Grave and Corporal Hebadiah Fetter. They were slaves to a tide of action, and they could only ride out the wave and see whither it took them. They had crossed some hurdles. Fat Simon was dead, as was Mathieu. They had made their landing and got into the castle. The drawback was that they were closely watched, de Poictiers was still highly suspicious, and there seemed no way they could make contact with Morkyn, the leader of the wolfsheads.

But, they were alive.

The great banqueting hall of Castle Falcon was a crowded, smoky place the next evening. All day the greatest lords of Sol Three had been arriving with their retinues, packing out every corner of the castle. In the confusion, Simon and Bogart had managed to both make themselves useful and still move around as much of the castle as possible. While they snatched a hunk of bread with thick white cheese, washed down with ale, they compared notes.

'The Armoury is strong enough. It would take a planned attack to bring it down. But, it seems vulnerable to fire. If the lower floor could be burned out, it would go hard on them to hold the rest. For all their strength. A careful blaze might force them back, yet leave a way open for a few determined men to get to the weapons. Simon, what wouldn't I give for a colt in my hand again. But I see no pheronium.'

'I have talked to other guards and they tell of the well-guarded quarry over towards Brakenham in the hills. May-be we must wait till our turn comes round. After the feasting tonight there is to be a conference in Mescarl's chambers. Just the nobles. No guard within the room. That, Bogie, is where one of us must be tonight.'

Tonight was come. They stood, a few feet apart, against the low balustrade of the gallery that ran round three sides of the hall. At the one end, opposite to them, a small group sang madrigals in high, clear voices – the voices of eunuchs – to the thin accompaniment of dulcimer and lute. Below, all was noise and confusion. The concealed power lights remained off, and the only relief from the dark was from an enormous fire in the hearth along one side of the room, as well as numerous glowing, spitting rush lights in sconces round the vaulted roof. At intervals, a serf would bustle about in the shadows with a long wooden ladder, trimming and replacing the torches as they guttered or went out.

The nobles and their immediate kin sat at the high table with Mescarl in the centre. It was an unusual feast, in that every lord and lady was of highest rank. The Baron himself looked about him like a fat lion, watching much, listening a great deal, but talking little. Beside him sat his albino son, face like a sun-bleached bone, eyes as red as the mouth of Hell. No wife lived, though Mescarl had wed thrice. None had brought him a child, apart from this cripple, Magus; all had died.

There were two other tables set at right angles from the main placing, where the lesser mortals sat, waiting on their lords to laugh. The stone floor was padded with a layer of clean rushes, now strewn with greasy bones, lumps of fat, crusts of bread, vomit and excrement. As the meal wore on, the nobility grew careless and found it too much trouble to stagger to the cold row of holes, hanging in space over the drop of the walls. Pots overflowed and finally they simply eased themselves where they sat.

Food lapped all over the tables. Boars' heads jostled capons, flesh ripped from their breasts to stuff red-lipped mouths. Plates of cold vegetables, slabs of venison, over-turned jugs of thick cream, plum tarts, crusted vats of soup all littered the benches and tables. Pages made a constant round with bowls of water and linen cloths for the guests to wipe their fingers and faces.

Goblets of silver and crystal, swilling over with dark Rhenish, sweet mead or simple ale were banged drunkenly on the plates, or rolled, neglected, to the floor. Beneath the tables dogs ran and fought, copulating with animals that the visiting nobles had brought. On the shoulder of Mescarl, aloof from this social maelstrom, sat a cat. Full black with a white ruff of fur round his neck, it was known as 'Priest', and treated with deference by every man and woman in Castle Falcon, for it was the Baron's favourite.

In the shadows of the hall, patient and unblinking, stood armed men, their hands resting easily on the hilts of swords. Watching the revelry and each other. For these were both the guards of Mescarl's household and of the visitors. If there were treachery, many of them had orders to first slay the Baron.

During the meal jongleurs and acrobats had competed with the food and drink as attractions. One unfortunate minstrel had failed to please the company and had been punished by having his tongue cut from his mouth. A lady present had won great applause, shouting out: 'Since his tongue did not agree with our digestions, let us see if it agrees with his!'

So the tongue was speared on a spit and thrust into the ashes at the edge of the fire, till it was well scorched. Then, covered in ashes as it was, it was cut into chunks and forced into the wretch's mouth by two of the lady's bully-boys. The crowd cheered and clapped, while the lady herself sat across from him and mocked his suffering. When it was over, the man was heaved into the moat, and his lute after him.

He drowned, which might have been the best for him.

Wrestlers, stripped naked, their bodies oiled, grappled in the centre of the hall, while the lords wagered on the winners. In his vantage point, Simon watched and remembered.

Though there were changes at Castle Falcon, many of them sinister and threatening, one thing had grown worse. The unspeakable cruelty of Baron Mescarl, and the pack of corrupted animals that fawned and frolicked about him. If these were the best and finest of Sol Three, then it was time for a purging. Sadly, cruelty on such a minor scale – even serfdom – was not enough justification for GalSec interference. Colonel Stacey's words came back to him about the fabric of the Galaxy being threatened. Simon clenched his fist on the wire-bound hilt of his broadsword and prayed, to whatever diety he cared for, that they might find the evidence that would enable him to take action. Then this rotten nest could be snuffed off the face of the planet.

He was so tense with his anger that he failed to notice someone at his elbow. 'You're Simeon Grave?'

'Yes, my lady. And you are the Lady Jocasta.'

In the hall there was the high crack of a bone snapping as one of the wrestlers won his victory. This led to an outburst of cursing and haggling from the winners and losers of the wagers. In the gallery Simon found himself being pushed gently into an angle, lost in deep shadow, back from the light.

'My lady, my duty is to my lord. I must watch.'

The eyes of the Lady Jocasta were very bright, flecks of red light glowing in them. Her mouth hung loose-lipped open, and her hand touched him on the thigh. 'No man here would dare harm Mescarl at this time. Not with his knowledge. He is safer here than he has ever been. Now, do you be quiet soldier, and let me have a little enjoyment. Mayhap, it could give you a little pleasure also.'

Her feral face was inches from his, and he steeled himself from recoiling from the odour of rotting teeth. She was not young; the wrinkled skin at the base of her neck, at the corners of her eyes and at the sides of her mouth placed her near to fifty. 'One word from me and your fate would be infinitely worse than that crook-voiced minstrel. It would not be your tongue that would be sliced off, Master Simeon, but *this*!'

Simon gasped as her nails dug through his breeches into his manhood. 'Stand still and say nothing, and you will have my protection in time of trouble.' She was very drunk, slurring her words and fumbling at the laces that tied up the front of his clothes. 'Be nice to poor Jocasta, and it may be that I can have you put to guard me. You would live in comfort. My chamber is close to that of the Baron, so your food would be of the best, and served warm. Just be nice.'

He did his best to stand still as she tore at him. When he was exposed, she dropped to her knees in front of him. By tremendous efforts of will, he was able to give her the reaction she wanted. Failure, he knew, would have been taken as a slight and punished accordingly. He even managed to smile to himself at the thought of Colonel Stacey's face if he were to tell him the lengths he was forced to; for the good of the service!

When she rose again to her feet, he was quick to tell her how wonderful it had been, and how much he appreciated the honour she had done him. 'If only, my lady . . . But, no. It could not be possible.'

Jocasta smiled at him, her mouth slipping uneasily near the edge of her face. 'What, my sweet soldier?'

'No, madam. My lord de Poictiers would forbid it.'

'That base dog! What would he forbid my champion?'

'It's just . . .' Simon swallowed hard. 'It's just that your champion would try another run in the lists with his lady.'

The Lady Jocasta simpered, tapping him on the cheek with a beringed finger. 'Rogue. I shall see to the old bear. You will come to my room in sixty minutes from now. Take this ring and the guards in the Falcon Tower will let you through.'

'But . . .'

'No buts. It is an order. Am I not the cousin of the all-powerful Baron Mescarl?' She hiccupped. 'As well as being the mother of that white . . .' She stopped; knowing even in her state of dreadful inebriation that she had said too much. The only safe thing to say in Castle Falcon was nothing. 'In one hour.' She pressed her ring into his hand, planted a wet kiss on his chin, and wandered off, humming a little song to herself.

Simon spat into the alcove behind him, relishing the relief from the taste of bile. A soft voice at his back made him jump. 'One of your most valuable assets is in danger of catching a chill.'

He quickly tucked himself back into his breeches and tied the laces. Then he turned to face Bogart with a wry grin. 'It was in the cause of GalSec service.'

'Aye. I'd not argue with the word "service"; though who was doing the servicing wasn't entirely clear.'

'Would it wipe that smile off your repulsive face if I told you she was the mother of Mescarl's whey-faced bastard. And that her room backs on to the conference chamber of the Baron.'

'The Lady Jocasta gets around. It fair made my loins tingle, watching her work on you. Why do these women go for runts like you? I don't get it.'

'There's more. I, Simeon Grave, am now the special guard to the Lady, with her seal ring to prove it. And I am to go to her within the hour. If any ask for me, I think it's better if you plead total innocence. Now back to your post. Hey! Wish me luck.'

'I would, sir. If I thought that you needed it.'

The hour before his tryst passed quietly enough. Many of the revellers had succumbed to the surfeit of drink, while some at the lower tables coupled shamelessly in the filth on the floor.

At the top table the visiting lords either dozed face-down in their unfinished meals or watched the entertainment. But the two or three nearest to Mescarl were more involved in a tight and urgent conversation. A conversation in which Mescarl himself took little part.

Because of the poor lighting Simon was unable to read what was going on – for a high degree of skill in lip-reading was an essential qualification for all active members of GalSec. Every now and then the Baron would nod, and Priest on his shoulders would rock a little to balance.

At his side, unmoving, sat Magus, the Baron's only misbegotten son. Even at that distance, Simon found it unnerving to see the way the red glow from the cressets was taken in and multiplied by his ruby eyes. The light burned from that skull of a face with a fearsome intensity, like the eyes at night of a carnivorous creature.

The banquet was clearly coming to its close. Most of the hangers-on were insensible and the senior lords were anxious for the talks to begin. But there was yet one more little treat to liven the jaded palates.

De Poictiers, who had stood unmoving through the long hours at the back of the hall, only leaving it to tour the castle or answer a call of nature, led in two men – one oldish and one a stripling. He announced that they were a father and son who had been caught trying to hamstring some of the lord's horses. The young one admitted that he was a follower of the renegade Morkyn. The old man, his father, had at first denied any involvement, but a little persuasion had changed his mind. Though he now said that he had been forced to do it for fear Morkyn came in the night as some hobgoblin and ripped out his throat.

Mescarl rapped on the table with the hilt of his dagger. 'Gentles! Attention! How shall we treat these scum?'

He got a drunken chorus of advice, ranging from burning to flogging, from mutilation to the rack. Simon tried to shut his mind off from the affair, for he could do nothing to aid the peasants. They were already as dead as if they had been decapitated an hour ago. But he looked up when a fluting reedy voice silenced the alcoholic shouts.

'Father, may I offer a suggestion?'

Mescarl nodded in surprise. 'Aye, Magus. What have ye in mind?'

'Let one die, and let the other go free.'

There was a murmur of surprise and dissent. One of the nobles at the top table – a very short man from the south, named Malan – spoke up. 'Pardon me, my Lord Magus.

But, would you let free a fox that you caught with a mouthful of your best cockerel?'

Magus bowed mockingly to Malan. 'If what I hear of your court is true, gentle lord, many a fine young cock thanks his saints each night that some old foxes have so few teeth.'

This sally brought a bellow of shocked laughter from Mescarl and a mixed reaction from the others. Malan himself flushed crimson and would have gone for his sword had not his neighbour restrained him. Simon noted that even a crippled lad might be a worthy opponent in some sports. The barbs in the remark were obvious, for he had noticed himself that Malan's retinue included a surprising number of beautiful young boys, who closed their eyes when they spoke, and whose breeches were a little too snugly cut.

Magus went on: 'What I suggest is this. Give them both a sword, and let one kill the other. It matters not which. The survivor shall go free.'

His father clapped him on the shoulder. 'I like it. By the mark of Cain, it shall be!! Seneschal, get them both a sword. There; you dogs, you understand?'

Both were freed from their bonds and handed swords. Without looking at his father the young man threw the sword across the room, where it lay in the rushes in front of Mescarl. 'You may kill us, but you will never turn us against one another. My lord, one day your infamy will come to the notice of some greater authority. Then will you . . .'

His words were cut short. Behind him, his father had taken the pommel of the sword like a drowning man grasping at a rope. Without a sound he had lifted it and thrust his son through the back, between the ribs on the left side. The boy cried out as he fell, though no man could tell what it was he cried.

The old man, sobbing and chattering, hacked at his son's corpse, tearing and mauling it as a wild animal might. He fell across it, still trying to stab it, until de Poictiers himself stepped forward and took the weapon from him, hauling him to stand in front of the Baron. The scene had been so grossly shocking that even that corrupt company had been silenced.

The only sound, apart from the heavy panting of the old man, was the thin giggling of the albino. The cat leaped down from his perch on Mescarl's shoulder and stepped delicately through the shambles on the stone floor. When he reached the body, he bounded softly over it and settled himself down on his haunches. Threads and rivulets of blood wound across the floor. The cat dipped his rough, pink tongue into one of these bright red pools and began to lap.

The sniggering increased. The old man looked at Magus, his old face working and jerking, like a ship's sail in a freshening wind. Every part of it seemed controlled by a different agent. 'I am to go free?'

Instantly, the laughter stopped, and that high, hateful small boy's voice spoke again. 'I gave my word. Take him away, wash him, feed him well and give him wine. Then let him sleep. Tomorrow, old man, when we all feel fresh, and the sun shines over this castle, and the birds swoop and cry about the battlements, and there is a sprightliness in the very air, you shall be brought to me again, and I will arrange for you to be set free. No harm will come to you. No hand will be laid on you. No man shall do you the least injury, lest he answer to me. I promised freedom to the winner. And you, are you not clearly the winner?' And again he slumped back in his seat, giggling.

Simon could wait no more. He shook off the shudders and left his post for the rooms of the Lady Jocasta. As he went, he pondered on how the frailest vessel could contain the most monstrous evil.

When he reached the heavily-guarded wing where members – those that had clung on to life – of Mescarl's family lived, Simon thanked his angel for Lady Jocasta's ring. Without it, one or two of the men-at-arms showed a distressing symptom of attacking first and asking the questions afterwards. Through barred gateways, studded doors and narrow passages that weaved and turned, giving one man a chance against many, the mediaeval lighting gave way gradually to modern concealed strips, though the stone walls remained massive and unyielding.

Finally, he reached the ornate ante-room of Lady Jocasta. A wrinkled duenna, her face locking away the secrets of too many ancient crimes, waved him through without even a glance at the proffered ring. But, as he was about to push through the tapestry that concealed the door to the suite, she called him back. 'The seal. In that dragon dish. If you need it again, she will arrange to get it to you. In the dish.' The voice was soft and tired, like dusty, old velvet.

He put the ring down as he was bid and walked through. He found himself in a large living-room with exactly the air of faded grandeur that he would have expected. Stuffed birds in glass domes jostled china animals missing legs or wings. All the furniture was over-stuffed and sagging. Smoke-darkened pictures hung on the walls, alternating with torn and faded tapestries of hunting scenes.

Over the cold fire-place, smeared where smoke-stains had been carelessly wiped off, was an oddly fascinating pointilliste portrait of a beautiful young woman. The paint shone through the dirt with a luminous quality that made it the centre of the sad room. Simon stood for a moment in front of the painting, holding the image of what Lady Jocasta had once been, before Castle Falcon made her what she was now. It would help him a little in what was to come. Remind him to be gentle. And so he turned from the room, realising what it had been in his cousin that had made Mescarl dare gossip and taboo. Despite the hag she now was, he could ever see why the Baron let her live.

He walked through to her sleeping-chamber, his feet making no sound on the thick-piled rugs. The room smelled heavy from drinking. The air was tired, weighted down with years of too much face powder and laboured lust. Across the huge bed sprawled the Lady Jocasta. Her hair was down, and she had managed to take off her dress, leaving her in a thin silk petticoat. She was asleep.

Everything told Simon to leave her quietly, but he could not. Only one wall away from him a conference was soon to take place that could, possibly, topple the whole Sol System.

Sitting down softly on the bed beside her, Simon stroked her hair. She stirred, like a child, and took his hand in hers and pressed it to her lips. Oddly moved, he leaned over her and brushed his lips to her cheek. Her arms went round his neck and pulled him down.

'You were kind, Simon.'

'Simeon. Simeon my lady, not Simon.'

'It matters not. You were kind to a sad old lady, and I thank you for it. There is so little kindness here. My cousin was always a monster, but he now has the power to make him uncontrollable. And my son . . . you will never speak of this, Simeon, it will mean both our heads?'

'My lady, I am as silent as the grave.'

'I care not. Death would be a welcome lover for me. I have lived too long and seen too much. Mescarl keeps my son – an unnatural and corrupt monster – and took away my little girl. She was killed, I have no doubt of it.' Tears began to furrow through the layers of paint and powder, peeling back the years. The wine she had drunk was almost gone, and the self-pity was becoming overwhelming, sparked by the unexpected kindness of a young soldier. 'She was a pretty little baby.' She began to sob in earnest. 'He used to come to me each night, and we would make love. I was hypnotised by him, as a trembling rabbit by a weaving serpent. It has been long years since he came. The key is long lost and the bolts are rusted.'

Simon held the old woman close and patted her back, as one does with a young child who has had a nasty dream. Putting his face closer, he whispered: 'How did the castle not know? Are there no sniffers, no sound bugs?'

'He would not have them here. So close to his own chambers. There was a time, after Robert and Ruth, and . . . Geoffrey – he was a handsome lad, Geoffrey, always a merry jest on his lips. He could stand in a clearing, still, and the birds would come to him. Would sit on his arms.'

There was a long quiet.

'What was I saying?'

'You were telling me of the castle after the accident.'

'Accident! It was bloody murder! But they are long dead. I would see Geoffrey again. It is the waiting, Simeon. Waiting each day. Aye, the castle. After the accident, Richard was aflame with suspicion. Every room had its own device. Each turn of the corridor its vid-scope. Informers flourished and many died, unnoted and alone, far below us. Now, he is secure. He needs no such tricks to keep his power.'

'But how did you meet? Would the servants not see you as you went to and from your trysts?'

She lifted her head from his shoulders and pointed across her room. 'There, behind the tapestry of Our Saviour showing His wounds to Doubting Thomas. There is a small door. It is probably still unlocked. It always was. Then a dark passage. No distance. I used to count the steps. Fourteen. Then his door. Now that is locked. I warrant he has forgotten it. For it too lies behind a picture. A hanging cloth of the Massacre of the Innocents.'

Again the Lady Jocasta began to weep, as old events and memories flooded her mind. 'Why do you not sleep, my lady? Let me caress you, and you will find the arms of Lethe wait to welcome you.'

She looked up at him. 'You are kind. I would we had met many years ago. Now, it is late. Too late. Too late. Too late. Aye, I would sleep. Will you come again? I beg you. I, the Lady Jocasta, beg you. Come to me tomorrow night. At the same hour. Please.' She smiled crookedly. 'That is a word that does not come easily to my tongue. You have given me kindness, Simeon. Do not hurt me by taking it away again. I do not think I could bear that. Will you come?'

'Aye, my lady. If I may.'

'You swear?'

'I swear.'

'Then help me to sleep.'

By putting his arms under her light body, it was an easy matter to lay her at ease in the bed. She kept her eyes closed as he lay out beside her, his fingers butterflying over her forehead. Soothing and caressing. Gradually he let his hands inch down towards her neck. Her breathing became more steady and regular; she was asleep.

Simon could hardly risk having Lady Jocasta wake while he was busy at his spying. He had to make sure she slept soundly. His fingers softly moved to a spot behind her right ear. Where a nerve and an artery are close together. He pressed accurately. Firmly. Blood slowed. The brain switched off some of its sections. The breathing thickened. Became quiet.

Until he came to apply a counter-pressure, the Lady Jocasta would sleep on. If he did not wake her, she would slumber until the body ran down.

Without a backwards glance Simon walked across to the tapestry of Doubting Thomas and slipped behind it. The dust billowed around him and he almost choked. Generations of beetles and spiders had lived and bred in solitude there, and hundreds of tiny, dried-up corpses crunched beneath his feet. The door was there. And it was open!

The rusted hinges scraped and did their best to prevent the hidden door from being forced open. To hush them, Simon used the temporary measure of dribbling spit on the most rusty parts. The tunnel was dank and cold. Nothing, not even the bravest mouse, had breathed in there for so many years. Fourteen of Lady Jocasta's bird-like steps were only worth eight of Simon's, and he was at the other door.

Not the least chink of light showed through, and Simon, even pressing his ear to the dry wood, could not hear the slightest sound. He took the spiralled metal ring that acted as a door-knob and slowly twisted it. His first reward was a piercing shriek of protest from the aged lock. Then he met resistance. The door *was* locked! Just the other side of it, nobles would be gathering – may already be gathered, may even be readying themselves, swords in hand, to rush through the betraying door and slaughter him where he stood. Simon began to sweat. He wiped his hands on his surcoat, and leaned his weight against the handle. Again the tearing sound of rotting metal met him.

'Turn you whoreson bastard bloody fugging drecky-poxed stinking . . . aaah!'

After so long without any movement, the tumblers of the lock had rusted into one another. There was no way that they could actually turn the lock; what could happen was what had happened. The ancient metal crumbled under Simon's pressure and the whole centre of the lock disintegrated. With a tug, the door opened a few inches.

No light and no sound!

He was still in time. Simon leaned against the rough wall and panted hard, eyes closed, perspiration streaming down his face. The effort had taken it all from him. His right arm tingled and shook. If there had been an armed man waiting for him, Simon could have done nothing. What he had seen and endured that night, combined with the fearful effort of opening the long-shut door, had taken all he had.

After a minute he straightened. Putting his hand round the edge of the door, he felt the rough material of the back of a tapestry. The tied knots hung limp to his touch. He knelt and reached for the bottom, and found it trailing safely to the floor. While he kneeled there, he caught the sound of mailed boots, the jingle of spurs, the clash of harsh voices. Quickly, he darted back and pulled the far door shut behind him. A trickle of light was finding its way into the passage; a rapid application of saliva to the hinges of Mescarl's door and he could push it nearly shut.

People filed into the chamber the other side of the Massacre of the Innocents and there was coughing, chair-scraping and shuffling that precedes any meeting. The muttering died away as someone – presumably Mescarl – thumped on the table.

'Order! Order! Let us get on.'

Another voice. Recognisable as the poisonous tones of Malan. 'Are we safe, my lord, from your damned sniffers?'

'Aye. What we say here will be heard by no man. You can speak with as much confidence as if you were in your own demesne.'

'Perhaps with more, father.'

Simon's eyes opened at that. Stacey had not mentioned the albino as being privy to any secrets. Yet he was there at the highest conference on the planet. When Simon had left Castle Falcon, there had been only rumours of the boy's existence. The putative mother had disappeared – a falling sickness had been the reason given out. Now Magus seemed a power to be counted.

After the initial pleasantries, the meeting carried on until the fourth hour of the morning, when they were all, more or less, in agreement. When the room was again dark and silent, Simon eased the door shut, retreated along the narrow passage, and closed the other end. He put Lady Jocasta back into a normal sleep and left for the guards' quarters. On the way out he took the seal ring from the dish and placed it in his pocket.

The crone waked at his passing, stirring in her chair. Her yellow eyes followed him across the room as incuriously as those of a sun-warmed lizard.

Despite all his training, Simon Rack found it impossible to calm his thoughts enough to get any sleep that night. There was too much to ponder.

Five
It Depends What You Mean By Living

None of the nobles, with the exception of the hard and indestructible de Poictiers, were up for matins. Though most of them surfaced to greet the midday meal. Some were to go hawking, and a party of guards was allocated to them. Simon learned that there was increasing concern in the castle at renegade activity, and it was felt that the brushwood folk might use the gathering of power to stage a major assault.

Neither Bogart nor Simon were included in the outside party – indeed, only those hand-picked by the Seneschal were thus trusted. For the rest of the garrison, it was confinement to castle duties for the eight days that the visitors were to stay.

The afternoon parade was the first time either of them had been outside that day, and they blinked in the strong sunlight. As they stood at ease, waiting for the inspection, they heard weak cries from somewhere above. Although they all craned their necks, whatever it was seemed just out of their sight.

When they were split up into platoons for the afternoon's duties, they found themselves at attention on the far side of the bailey. They could then see the source of the noise. Hanging from a chamber near the top of the Falcon Tower was a large, black iron cage. Made of bars of iron set a few centimetres apart, the cage pitched and swung as the breeze caught it. Inside, slumped in a corner, was the old man who had slain his son in the banqueting hall the previous night.

A soldier next to them nodded up at the dangling prison. 'I'll say that for white-face. He always keeps his word. Promised the old man he could live and that no man would harm him. So, there he'll swing, safe as houses. Though he seems to be wanting for water already, and it ain't that hot. By tomorrow it'll be food he'll cry for. Though, without any clothes, and him being a real dotard, he may not make it through the night.'

Bogart spat out of the corner of his mouth, on to the cobbles, narrowly missing the soldier's feet. 'Aye. He's a skilful way with words. And his mercy! I have seen a crazed rat with more.'

Simon nudged him, to shut him up, but de Poictiers appeared at that moment and called them to order, ending possible trouble.

The wretch hung for three days, before all movement finally ceased. Two days later, the cage was removed. The room from which it had been hung was the bed-chamber of Magus Richard Mescarl!

The day passed quietly. That night, after they had been stood down, Simon sat with Bogie as they burnished their swords and explained his plan. He wasted no words.

'One. We've got eight days. Two. At the end of that time all these fine folk will be back to their own demesnes and the chance is gone. Three. If we could reach GalSec we could have a star-ship here in a day. Four. Since we had to destruct our ship, there is no way we can get through to GalSec. The only transmitters are so guarded it's impossible to get at them. Five. That means it's down to us. We have to reach Morkyn, convince him of the urgency of things and lead an attack on Castle Falcon.'

'We've no chance of getting out. De Poictiers sees to that. So, here we are and here we rest.'

'Wrong. Tonight, after I've seen poor old Jocasta, I'm going to try for a break. You'll have to stay and look as innocent as you know. I'll make for the woods and Morkyn.'

'How much will you tell him?'

'The truth. That Mescarl leads a cabel of Sol Three lords each of whom has a strong interest in the pheronium supplies to the Federation. That they each have arranged to build up their supplies by pressing peasants into slavery in their mines. Then, the pheronium will be taken to secret hiding-places all over the world. The next shuttle to call at the port will carry back nothing more than a crudely-worded ultimatum.'

'A damned ransom.'

'Aye. Freedom within the Federation. Acceptance of slavery. A ten-fold price for the ore. And power. Power over not only Sol Three but over the whole Sol System.'

'Without the pheronium every star-ship will be useless within weeks. Any attempted retribution and all the supplies will be destroyed. God knows there's little enough of the stuff anyway. And it can't be synthesised.'

Simon slammed his sword down on his bed. 'And the only men who know of this are all here in this one place. If they are to be thwarted, we must take this place and hold them. So, tonight I try. I'd go earlier, but Lady Jocasta would raise a fuss if I didn't go. Then all would be up. She seems to have taken to me as her last chance in life. It will come as a sad blow when I reveal myself.'

Bogie laid his polished blade across that of Simon. 'Take care. If you are caught, they will watch me with double caution.' He glanced at the large master-clock in the corner of the bleak barrack-room. 'Come on Corporal Simeon. Time for a last bite in the refectory. Then you may be off. Perhaps a drop of this awful piss they call small beer to boost your passion for her ladyship.'

The castle was quiet as he set out, Lady Jocasta's ring firmly in his fist. In the distance, echoing through the stone corridors, he could hear the measured tread of patrols. There was no banquet that night, though numbers of young girls from Standon, Brakenham and even further off had been brought to the castle in covered carts. From their reaction, when they found themselves in the inner bailey of Castle Falcon, not all came willingly.

Simon stepped softly past closed doors, towards the family suites. He had just reached a junction of passages when someone struck him neatly over the back of the head with something soft and flexible.

It was by no means the first time he had been knocked unconscious. As usual, his first thought as he began to come round was how wrong most writers were. There were no stars, no flashing lights, no ringing bells. It was as though someone had thrown an off-switch in the brain; no intermediate stage. A measureless time floating alone in the centre of one's skull. Then a slight sickness and a pain behind the eyes that means you are getting over it. The other fallacy was that a man could have such control over his body that he was able to hide the fact that he was coming round. If you were really knocked out, you came round when your brain let you, not before.

Simon opened his eyes painfully, to gaze into the light of torches. He was held firmly by the arms. Two men behind him, one to each arm. In front, a ring of lights – six, eight – and closest of all, a bearded man's face. De Poictiers.

'Well, well, well. No promotion for you, Corporal Grave. Out of quarters . . . I know your damned face. From a long time ago . . . It will come. You were out of quarters. Why?'

A shaking of his head cleared his thoughts a little. Careful! 'I was on my way to the rooms of the Lady Jocasta.

To guard her through the night. As I did yesterday. As I think you know, my lord?'

De Poictiers was smiling behind his beard. 'I have a vague recollection of some such request. If you are for the Lady, then you will carry her seal. All of her . . . "guards" . . . are given one.'

So that was it! They hadn't trapped him as a spy. It was merely a trick of de Poictiers to maintain his own discipline. When he was struck down, he had obviously dropped the ring. By now it was safely in the purse of the Seneschal. Well, it was hard. But, it would pass. 'I had it, my lord,' he said, choosing his words with care. 'But, perhaps I may have dropped it. If your lordship would allow me to go on my way, then the Lady Jocasta will vouch for my words.'

De Poictiers thrust his face closer. His beard brushed Simon's face as he spat out his glee. 'No! Impudent cur! You have no seal. Therefore you are a liar. I, I say that you lie. I say that you have crept out of your quarters for some shabby coupling with a drab from the skullery. I say that you will be chained up in the guard-room for four days on bread and water. I say that your sneaking comrade will mew you up himself. That way, both of you will be out of my way for a little. What say you to that?'

There was little he could say. Except that the Lady was waiting for him. If he were any judge of women, she would take it sore if he did not attend on her. He had no chance to frame a reply. The Seneschal had stepped back and was smiling at him fondly.

'Good Simeon, I vow you look less than well. It is a distance to the guard-house and I would not have you tired by walking the hard cobbles.'

And he nodded to one of the men behind Simon. He had only time to screw up his eyes – which does not do the least good but is a primitive reaction to an inevitable accident –

when everything again turned off. He floated for a long time.

When he sank back to normality, it was with what seemed an agonisingly painful stiff neck. A brief exploration revealed the pain came from a metal collar, rough-edged, bolted at the back. The stiffness was a result of the collar being attached to a chain which was, in turn, stapled to the wall. The cell wall.

He lay on straw, and it was coming light. Unlike the deep dungeons, this cell was in the guard-house and had a barred window that overlooked the inner bailey. There was a hiss from the door. With a struggle, Simon managed to focus on the grille in the centre. There, looking worried and miserable, was half the face of Bogart.

It seemed that de Poictiers had kept his word. Simon was on bread and water for four days for neglect of duty. His guard, with six hours on and two off, was Corporal Hebadiah Fetter.

After matins the Seneschal came to visit the prisoner. Strangely, he seemed uneasy. He paced about the small cell, flicking with his foot at bits of straw. Finally, he went to the window and hung his arms through the bars, talking to Simon over his shoulder.

'You puzzle me, Master Grave. There is much about you to set me wondering. You and your ill-mannered comrade arrive on Sol Three, landing near Castle Falcon just before the most important gathering of nobles for decades. You claim to be mercenary soldiers. The way you escaped the Worm's Lair makes me think that could be. Also, both of you have a way with yourselves. A confidence in bearing. Your ship mysteriously burns up. There is a brawl in a dello with men killed. One of them a suspected wolfshead. You take up with the Lady Jocasta.

You sneak about the castle late at night. No, don't interrupt me. I know your tale, and I am now inclined to believe it. Here, take this. She will not need it.'

He threw something into the straw near Simon and turned back to gaze from the window. Leaning forwards, pulling against the chafe of the iron, Simon scrabbled in the straw.

De Poictiers spoke again. 'Then there was the death of Mathieu. Again, both of you were there. A load of odd coincidences, sirrah. You must admit. But, that ring is evidence of some truth. What happened this morning is greater proof.'

Simon held the seal ring of the Lady Jocasta Mescarl. 'What has happened to her?'

The Seneschal turned back. 'She is dead. Your friend will doubtless tell you of it. I will not. For my part I am glad of it, for it was a release. Once I . . .' He stopped. 'I must believe she cared for you. Otherwise . . .' Having said enough, he strode back to the door and swung it open. 'One last word. When I recall your face, it may go ill, or it may go well. Until then, you will be freed on the morrow. Then you may resume your duties.'

The heavy door slammed shut.

It was not until afternoon that Bogie was able to get in to tell him what had happened. It was a short and sad tale.

Lady Jocasta had waited long for Simon. She had twice sent her old maidservant to look for him. Each time she could not find him. Finally, she had dismissed her and shut herself in the bedchamber. In the morning, the woman had entered to wake her mistress and found her dead. She had taken her dress-making shears and cut a long strip from one of her sheets. By climbing on a lacquered table, she had managed to tie the one end to a hanging sconce. The other end she had looped round her thin neck.

Then, like a swimmer entering deep water, she had slipped to her ending.

'Truly, I am sorry, Bogie. But, she was very tired.'

'Aye. They say that Magus laughed when he heard the news.'

'That red-eyed bastard builds up a score that will be hard to settle. But, I may yet manage it.'

Five of the eight days had gone. The old man and his cage were removed. The frail body of the Lady Jocasta was laid to rest, with Simon as a pall-bearer at her funeral. The man who linked arms with him at the front of the ornate coffin was de Poictiers. As they carried her to the family vault, through the inner bailey, Magus sat in his casement and blew rainbow bubbles into the warm air. Some burst, while others rose and flew high over the walls of the keep.

On the sixth day, Mescarl sent for Simon. 'Corporal Grave, I hear from the good de Poictiers that you and your friend are having ups and downs since you came so miraculously to us. Perhaps you are too cribbed up. I have persuaded him that you should ride out with us today. I take my guests to visit the quarry. It is a long ride and will take much of the day. But your short friend will stay here. Only, you understand, so that we may be assured that you will not only ride out with us. You will also return. You do understand, don't you?'

Simon stood rigidly at attention. 'Yes, my lord. I understand you perfectly.'

Mescarl smiled. He wore court mourning, as did all the nobles. Though, Magus wore his black in a way that contrived to mock the dignity. The Baron wore a vast cloak of black silk, that rustled and chattered as he moved. Atop one shoulder lay the cat, Priest, his white collar a startling flash in all the sable.

'Very well. We leave in the hour.'

It was a long and winding procession that clattered over the drawbridge of Castle Falcon. Lords pranced on their stallions, while ladies rode more sedately on richly caparisoned palfreys. An advance squadron, mixed from the troops of the visitors and Mescarl's own elite, rode a hundred metres ahead of the main body. Other soldiers ranged to right and left, while the main body, led by de Poictiers, followed close behind.

Altogether, there were some two hundred souls. The plan for the day was that the morning was to be spent in hawking and hunting. After the midday meal, most of the troops would escort the ladies back to the castle. The remainder would move on to the pheronium quarries and processing plant.

Simon rode in the first rank of the rear-guard, just behind de Poictiers. He wore full mail – a long coat that reached below the knees – and a steel cap. Apart from the long sword, he still carried one of his stubby, leaf-bladed throwing knives in its doeskin pouch at the back of his neck. It was a hot day.

There were too many for the falcons to do their work well; jesses tangled and birds even stooped at one another. Many a lady forgot herself in the heat and the chaos, and the language grew more like a market-day stews than an outing of the nobility.

Mescarl led a few men in a half-hearted attempt to ride down a handful of boars that had been trapped and were released by serfs as the lords approached. But the 'holloas' and shouting lacked spirit. The sun grew higher and warmer in a clear, towering sky of deep blue. Some of the beasts were so confused that they stood still while they were ridden down with the long boar-spears.

One old brute, with wicked, curving tushes, darted red-eyed through the foot soldiers, ripping the stomach of one poor fellow who stumbled in its path. De Poictiers wheeled his horse to check it, when the boar swerved on the charge, catching the foreleg of the stallion and brought it crashing to the ground.

Ladies screamed as the beast whirled and faced the fallen horse. The knight was trapped by the leg and could only look on helplessly as his death pawed the ground in its murderous rage. Then it charged. None of that fine nobility did aught to help the Seneschal.

Simon wished for the man's death. But this was not an old man, past his prime and prematurely crippled like Mathieu. De Poictiers was still a fine man, a figure to be admired, proud and arrogant, who would step aside for no person but his sworn lord. It was not meet that he should die, torn apart by a wild pig. That would not satisfy Simon.

With a wild yell he spurred his own horse forward, but the beast reared and threw him awkwardly. However, the distraction had checked the boar, and it needed a moment to build up again to its charge. In that moment Simon had put himself in its path.

Kneeling on one knee, the butt of the spear lodged on the ground behind him, almost touching the struggling, cursing Seneschal, one hand near the knee to steady it, the other higher up the shaft, near the cross-piece, to brace it, he ignored a yell from the man behind him and waited.

All around him there seemed to be a shambles of noise and activity. Then, as he gazed into the eyes of the boar, all that faded away and his attention crystallised on the animal. Like a moment frozen in a silver ball, there was only the boar and he in all the world. It began to move and it was all in slow motion. Turves flew from its heels, bounding about it. The ground shook. He watched, fascinated, as the shoulder muscles rippled with the effort of movement, coarse hair bristling. Its tusks, one longer than the other, yellowing and stained with its rooting. Red smears on the left side from its recent killing.

Blood seemed to roar in his ears with the tension. Adrenalin pumped into his system. Then there was a shattering crash that threw him on his back as the point of his spear caught the charging boar clean through the breast bone. Had it not been for the cross-piece, the beast would have ripped its way clear through the spear and savaged him as it died.

While he hung on to the bucking spear, the boar's snout was only inches from his groin. Its breath foul in his face as it snorted hatred. Then, there was a gout of thick blood from its open jaws and it was dead.

After the exclamations and the applause had abated, after he had received kisses from the ladies and gifts of rings and gold from the men – including a handsome blood opal from Mescarl – he stood alone for a moment with de Poictiers.

His hands shook as he supped a goblet of wine, handed to him by the white-faced Seneschal. The bigger man put his hand on his shoulder and walked him a little away from the throng.

'First, I thank you. I owe you what I have owed few men ever before. You saved my life. The boar would have rended me before any other had thought to move. Nay, protest not. Hear me out, for there is more. You have my thanks. It places me heavily in your debt. This is something I do not much like. But never was a debt more speedily paid. When we return to Castle Falcon tonight, I will arrange for you and your friend to be well-mounted and given food. I can explain it away. You will ride out and you will never return. Go safely back to your friends of Galactic Security. Go away again and this time stay away, Simon Rack.'

It had always been a risk, Simon would have been the first to admit that. Although the check had only revealed three men still alive at Castle Falcon who knew him at all well, there was still the possibility that some serving-girl might recognise him. Time had wrought many changes in him, but the essence of the man he had become must have been there in those days. He had been lucky that fat Simon had died in the blazing scout. The killing of Mathieu had been more planned, but luck had still thrown her dice in his favour. Now the odds had turned. The sand had run out. Both lares and penates had chosen to turn their backs. Use what concept you like.

Yet, even now, there was still an outside chance. With de Poictiers so in his debt – and he was a man of honour who would stick rigidly to the letter of his promise – it left Simon two choices. If you count the mild acceptance of the offer and the concomitant abandonment of his mission, then he had three choices. But, in reality, that third choice was no choice at all.

So he could try and slay de Poictiers, and silence him for ever. Or he could run for the woods and try and find Morkyn. That would mean abandoning Bogie. No, it had to be a killing.

When the Seneschal faced him with his knowledge, Simon found himself with nothing to say. De Poictiers' eyes rested on him coldly. 'If it were not for the debt, I would cut you down where you stand. You know that?'

People were beginning to drift over to them again.

'Aye, my lord. I know you well enough for that. As to the saving of your life, I would not let you die while I looked on. I have waited long for such a day, but that was not behovely. As to your words, I will think on them well this day. And, my lord, I in my turn thank you.'

But circumstances reduced Simon's options to one. The fall had injured de Poictiers's ankle and the Baron ordered him back to the castle with the ladies. Simon, instantly promoted by Mescarl to sergeant, was to remain with the nobles and lead the advance guard to the quarry.

He watched the straight back of the Seneschal as he led away the large guard party and the bright array of the ladies. Simon tugged at the reins of his horse and moved off in the opposite direction. His lips barely moved and not even the nearest man caught the whisper. 'Sorry, Bogie.'

The trek to the quarry was long and sombre for Simon, though Mescarl and the nobles were in good humour. Their plans were nearing completion and wealth and power beyond any bounds were theirs to take and hold.

It was a long and hard ride, often through thick woods and high ravines. Excellent ambush country. Three times as they neared the mining area arrows whirred from the shadows. One soldier was struck through the throat and died quickly. A second shaft wounded the horse of one of the nobles, and a third feathered itself in the soft ground just in front of Simon's horse.

While Mescarl took his guests on a personally conducted tour of the mine, Simon placed the men in a ring around the top of the quarry. Twice men reported seeing movement below them, but there was no attack. The mine was a scar on the land, gaping open.

From his position Simon could not see as much as he would have liked of the mining activities. But he could see that the men who dug and hacked at the compressed layers of the ore-bearing strata were in poor physical condition. That they wore iron neck-rings. That they were chained together in pairs. That they were prodded to work with the butt-end of spears and vicious leather whips. That they were not even serfs. Reports had been true; Mescarl had indeed reintroduced slavery.

With one eye on the woods at the base of the hill, Simon watched the fat black figure of the Baron as he skipped through the dust at the bottom of the quarry. One thing surprised him. Pheronium was in short supply, and this was one of only a dozen places where it had been found on all of Sol Three. Mescarl's processing plant was the largest in the hemisphere and the space shuttles constantly thundered over as they carried refined pheronium from the planet to large space freighters waiting above the atmosphere in orbit.

This quarry was to the south of the castle, yet reports reaching Stacey had told of men and guarded wagons vanishing into the wasteland to the north. Old maps showed that region to have been the site of a huge megopolis before the wars. The fission and neutronic explosions that came close to wiping out the planet had rended the earth and wreaked dreadful changes in the very structure of the rock. One of the by-products of this was the reactive ore, phenonium. A substance that kept space vessels flying throughout the Galaxy.

The site of the old city, far in the misty hills to the north, would be a place where you might expect to find traces of ore. Yet, the mine was to the south. And a small mine. It wasn't impossible that Mescarl was playing a deeper game than anyone suspected. That he was ready to double-cross his allies and take everything. The realisation of that sent a chill down the base of Simon's spine. If that was right, he was a senior officer in the exclusive guard of the putative dictator of the Galaxy!

That train of thought was interrupted by a call from one of his men. Simon half-slid, half-ran down through the sandy slope and grabbed at his shoulder to save himself from slipping further. 'I . . . I'm not absolutely sure, Simeon, but I could have sworn I saw a large body of men between those two hills. There. Like a little column of ants. It's difficult to tell at this distance.'

Simon shaded his eyes and peered out where the man pointed. There were certainly no men there now, but there did seem to be a faint haze of dust hanging in the air. Another soldier joined them. 'Pardon me, sergeant. But if Wat here reckons that he saw some men, then I reckon he did. He's got an eye like a gyrfalcon.'

'All right, Wat, how many?'

'Difficult. Maybe fifty. Could be as many as a hundred.'

'God's wounds, man! A hundred! Over there on our way back to the castle.'

Sweat starting inside his leather vest, Simon bounded, uncaring of safety, down to the bunch of nobles. It was ironic, he thought, that he should be doing his best to try and save Mescarl from the brushwood men. But if that number attacked, it was likely that they would kill all the nobles. Worse, there was a grave risk that they might kill him. Then, with Bogart as good as dead, there would be nobody left to carry the torch.

The Baron was little worried and seemed to think that Simon was exaggerating the numbers. 'My dear Grave, these wolfsheads scarcely number a hundred, counting in every man, woman, dotard and puking brat. But we have done here, so we will leave. Close order, I think. And it might be better if we avoided that defile. Go the eastern route. Since you are strange to the area, let Sergeant Brooke lead the advance. You will guard the rear. Gentlemen, we will return to the castle!'

Mescarl may not have been worried, but some of his

friends were less sure. They crowded together in the centre of a ring of steel, casting nervous glances about them. Simon rode last of the company, one hand on the reins, the other resting on the pommel of his sword. As the party entered a rocky defile, a flock of swallows rose from the trees ahead, rising like tiny sickles on a gentle thermal. For a second or two he had space to wonder what had put the birds up. Then, sudden as a peal of thunder from a summer sky, his horse fell from under him. As he rolled free of the threshing beast, he saw the broken stump of an arrow protruding from the jagged wound behind its left shoulder.

Other shafts hummed through the air, and he dropped to one knee, sword ready. He glimpsed the soldier named Wat hanging low in the saddle, galloping for the woods, waving and shouting at the hidden bowmen. So the 'Maybe fifty. Could be as many as a hundred' was a lie and the wolfsheads had reached close to the throne.

Many were down, and men in rough green and brown jerkins were crawling forward with long thin knives to poke through helms and slit throats. Although the party was in a shambles Mescarl showed his mettle as a leader. He waved his huge sword over his head in one hand and screamed at his men to rally on him. Twice an arrow glanced off his armour; once a couple of the attackers broke cover and zig-zagged through the plunging mêlée to try and gut his horse. The Baron saw them coming and cut both down with absurd ease.

No others showed themselves and, gradually, order reasserted itself. Sparing no thought for the fallen, most of the nobles and twenty or so soldiers galloped off through the ravine, heads down to avoid the stinging swarm of arrows that followed them.

There was a pause. Simon risked all and stood; suddenly and deliberately threw his sword on to the ground. Around him two or three wounded men moaned, and one of the horses screamed thinly, its foreleg splintered by a fall. Gradually, in ones and twos, the renegades came out from their cover. Some kept arrows ready notched to their strings, but it was soon obvious the fracas was over. One went with sword in hand amongst all the fallen, cutting the throats of every man and beast on the ground. Taking no chances. Soon the groans and the horses' screams were still.

It was not a time to talk. Simon was the only survivor. A wrong word and there might not be any survivors. There were some edgy bow-fingers around. While he was watched, a conversation went on among a group of men just on the edge of the forest.

Three of them, Wat, an old man and a huge fellow built like a granite wall, came over to him. The big man spoke first. 'Sergeant Simeon Grave. Wat and my uncle are for slitting your gizzard here and now. I say that you may have an interesting tale to tell us. What do you say?'

'I say that I would talk. But I would only talk to your leader. Where is Morkyn?'

Wat stepped forward and spat in his face. 'Learn to guard your tongue, friend Simeon! You don't have the protection of the great and kindly Baron Mescarl to shelter you. It is not for you to say when you will and when you will not talk. Now you are with the free men of the woods. One word amiss and your blood with soften this sandy soil.'

Simon lifted a gauntlet and wiped away the thin string of spittle from his cheek. 'You talk to me of your freedom. A traitor who leads men to their deaths. Men he called friends an hour before. Unless your leader gives you leave to slay me, Wat, you must never leave your back unguarded. For I will kill you for that insult.'

Wat's hand flashed to his knife and slashed at Simon's

throat. He swayed back from it and began to move in, but the big man reached out and held them apart. The hand that grasped Simon's jerkin was hard as an oaken board and large as a shank end of mutton. For a moment he actually lifted both Simon and Wat, who was no stripling, off their feet.

'You, Wat, have done well this day. But collect your wits and think on who in this band decides life and death. As for you, lackey, you were never closer to death than that moment. You had one foot on Hades' further shore.'

Simon had already decided that weakness and compromise would be pointless with these folk. So he shook off the great fist. 'Morkyn, for so you must be, I think that you are become an old woman. You think you saved *my* life! That fool there would be dead by now. Treat me not like a fool, for we have a common aim. But if you would have me killed, then let your bowmen shoot me down while I am held. For if any man comes against me I will slay him.'

The old man laughed and clapped his wrinkled hands. 'Well said! I have long thought these pups needed a lesson. But mark well, it is the rules that any man may challenge another. But the winner must face Morkyn.'

This was the crunch. 'What if I would challenge Morkyn?'

'If you win, then you are the leader.'

Morkyn bellowed his merriment. 'Aye, and boars may fly to the sun with jewelled rings in their ears. Enough of this foolishness. Let us go.'

The fallen were soon plundered and the men moved away, leaving their own dead with those of the castle. It was a long walk and it was made in total silence. Morkyn stalked ahead, and Simon was surrounded by wolfsheads, swords drawn. His hands were tied and his eyes wrapped with a rag. It was a vast relief when they finally reached their destination. The scarf was torn from his face by the rough hand of Wat, and he blinked into the light of a fire. Round him stood a mute throng of men, women and children, with their mud and wattle hovels ringing them. Wat grinned at the look on Simon's face. 'Well, 'tis not the luxury you had expected, dead man. You'll have no silken sheets here, no fine food. No rich wine. But the air you breathe will be free – not tainted with slavery.'

Ignoring him, Simon looked round. Mescarl had not been far wrong in his guess at their numbers. Despite their wretched appearance, most seemed healthy, and the ambush had not been badly executed. For the first time, his vague plans began to assume a glow of possibility.

He waited for a few minutes, and was then led into the largest of the huts – obviously Morkyn's. The crowd had not moved, not shouted at him, talked, thrown anything at him. Just watched. There seemed no hatred, just a crippling apathy.

It was gloomy inside the hut, and he could just make out the looming figure of Morkyn, sprawled on a pile of stinking skins. Sitting beside him was a woman. Standing to one side was the old man, with Wat and two others of the fighting party. Simon stood before them.

'I think you may be a man I've awaited. If you are, then you can give me some clue. If you are not, then you'll not even know what I speak. Well?'

'How do you know you have no spy here?'

Morkyn sat up, and his voice became angry. 'I know who I can trust and how far I can trust them. No man here would betray me.'

'Not him?' pointing at Wat. 'Already today he has led men he knew to their deaths. Once a traitor, perhaps always a traitor. I am the man you have awaited, but I will only talk to you.'

'I could find a way of making you loosen that stubborn

tongue. But I see no reason to. If ye be who ye say, it will be well. Leave us.'

There was some grumbling, notably from Wat, but the hut emptied. Except for the woman. Simon pointed at her without speaking. She stood and walked to face him. She was little shorter than him, with a lithe, pantherish grace that he had not seen from any woman since he came to Sol Three. Her hair was a cascade of black water, tumbling over her shoulders. Though her skin was roughened by exposure to wind and sun, she was still a truly beautiful woman. As she stood close to him, her breasts almost brushing his chest, he felt his pulse quicken.

'I am Guenara. I am the woman of the leader.'

Morkyn interrupted her. 'You are mine.'

She did not turn her head to answer him. Her deep eyes remained locked with Simon. 'I said I am the woman of the leader. As you are the leader, then I must be your woman. As such I stay for all councils. All.'

There was little point in arguing, and time was running too short for Simon to want to waste any of it. So in that smoky hut, with wooden bowls of thick vegetable soup on their laps, they talked.

And talked.

Simon Rack was no fool and spent much of his time in the company of liars and rogues. He had a keen sense of smell for the phoney and the false. Something was wrong about Morkyn. Just what it was, he couldn't pin down. The man was the leader of the guerrilla group opposed to Mescarl, yet he greeted Simon's words with scant enthusiasm. On the surface he was all fire and eagerness. But Simon felt that there was little beneath to back it up. He prevaricated so much that Simon finally tired of it.

'Morkyn. Talk is cheap. The price of action comes a deal higher. Hours pass while we talk here. In Castle

Falcon, a friend of mine will soon be dying. I would not wish that happen for nothing.'

The big man rose grudgingly to his feet and walked to the hut door. He peered outside into the darkness for a few moments without speaking. Then, muttering something about 'a word with my lieutenants', he left.

Simon angrily threw the remainder of his mug of sour milk into the fire, so it hissed and spat, filling the room with the smell of burning. The woman had hardly opened her mouth during the hours of discussion, and she still sat, a feline shadow, in one corner. Morkyn's footsteps faded away.

The silence was suddenly filled with her voice. Low and urgent. 'He is foresworn. To Mescarl. Only I know this, but I can see far into the mind of men, and I see that you also suspect this. That is why he will not move. He looks for any excuse. For a way of not fighting.'

'Why? And when? We heard the request first from him. He was my main – my only – chance. How can he be a traitor?'

She beckoned Simon to sit beside her. 'I tell you this because I believe what you have said. Morkyn will never help you. He will place all manner of obstacles in your path. Since he is the leader, all the group will follow him. Even if I back you, it will help little. His reason for betrayal is an old one. Mescarl has promised him a position of power if he aids him. I know this for he has recently mentioned that the day will come when I stand as high as any lady.'

'But when? It must have been recent. Wait . . . wait a minute. With his plans coming so close to completion, Mescarl could not afford any tiny mishap. Nothing could go wrong that might affect the balance of his scheming. Now, he knew about Morkyn and this party. If he'd wanted, he could probably have mounted a force and crushed them. But, he might have failed. You all know this area, and even a large and well-armed power can fail against well-led guerrilla bands. History, especially the history of this planet, is full of such cases. So, what can he do? Infiltrate. Get his man at the top. Morkyn is the top man, so Mescarl reaches him. That way, he knows that the wolfsheads will do nothing likely to upset his plans. Hell's blood!!'

'I fear, Simon, that there is nothing you can do. If you attempt to leave, he will kill you as a traitor. If you remain silent, then he will make sure that the plans move forward so slowly that events will pass us by. I would have bitten out his throat as he lay with me had I known time was so against us. I am sorry.'

'Perhaps. Perhaps not, Guenara. What I cannot understand is the cunning of the plan. Many years ago I knew Mescarl. He was a bluff, hearty, ruthless, ambitious and cruel man. Braver than many a dictator and more stupid than most. Yet, each turning of the maze reveals a devious mind. At each step he has seen ahead to the possible danger and he has taken cunning steps to remove the danger. Mescarl would have charged in here like an old woman with a kettle of hot water trying to destroy an ants' nest. And, like an old woman, he would have killed some, while the rest hid and reappeared later, stronger than ever.'

'It was not the Baron who came to Morkyn. It was another.'

Simon looked at the woman with amazement. 'You saw them together! When?'

'About two months ago. Morkyn had got up in the night and left me. I thought he had gone to make water, but I heard him putting on his clothes. I was suspicious and followed him. He went by a secret path to a clearing near a small waterfall. I was able to come close through the underbrush. He talked for a time with a small man in a heavy cloak.'

Simon grabbed her by the shoulder, digging his fingers in hard. 'What was he like?'

They both heard steps coming back towards the hut – the weighty steps of a big man. Guenara drew away from him, rubbing at her arm. 'His voice was soft and high for a man. As wicked as a scorpion in a flask of honey. And, when he walked, he dragged one leg.'

'Of course. White-faced Magus!'

At that moment, Morkyn towered into the hut. In his hand he held a large burning torch.

Six
Meanwhile, Back At The Castle . . .

The worst of it was that there could be no relaxation. If he tried to stand upright, he cracked his head on the low vaulting. If he attempted to sit down, or lie, the iron round his neck first galled, then strangled. So it meant a cramped, bending position. His hands were manacled so tightly that a thin trickle of blood ran from under the bruised nails. His feet were free and he shuffled them now and again in the straw to keep at least one part of his body functioning.

First the ladies had returned, full of praise for the brave Sergeant Grave. With them had come de Poictiers, limping slightly from an ankle injury. The castle was soon abuzz with news of the killing of the boar and the rapid promotion of the Baron's new favourite.

An hour or so passed and then the guard on the watch-tower hallooed news of another party. The Baron, most of the nobles and the bulk of his guard, horses lathered, some with arrow wounds, riding furiously for the gates. They clattered into the inner bailey, shouting and cursing the brushwood men and their treachery. Bogart saw with mixed feelings that Simon was not with the party. Though several had seen him fall, one man said he thought he saw him roll safely when his horse went down. Long association with Simon Rack had given Bogie implicit faith in his powers of survival. Perhaps, even, the whole thing had somehow been stage-managed by Simon as a ruse to link up with the wolfsheads.

When he went off duty, later that afternoon, Bogart was

in a good mood. It seemed as though Simon had cleverly pulled off what he wanted, without jeapardising his position at the castle. Indeed, many of the other nobles were pressing for a sally to try and aid the fallen hero. Mescarl had gone first to the rooms of de Poictiers, and had not come out for over an hour. When he did, it was to call a conference of the major nobles.

Bogie was aware of this, but there was nothing he could do about it, so he simply went to the drinker – reserved only for corporals and sergeants – and began an evening's light drinking. For most men the amount of ale he consumed would have sent them crying for ice and a darkened room. By early evening he was merely jocund.

He raised and lowered his eyelids, trying to clear his brain and work out what had happened. He had been called to de Poictiers's chambers, and had gone there expecting some solicitous words for the loss of his friend. Instead he was slapped hard in the face with a mailed glove, knocked to the floor with a blow to the head and then kicked repeatedly in the body until he slipped away into a void.

Then, there he was, all chained up in one of the upper dungeons. He could tell roughly where he was because it was not quite dark and the ribbed patch of light sky stood out against the blackness of the cell.

Later that same night he was stripped and taken to what was only too obviously the torture chamber of Castle Falcon. He was laid, face up, on a table greasy with old sweat and blood, and rank with the stench of fear. His hands were manacled to the top corner of the table, while his ankles were drawn painfuly apart and secured to the oposite corners. By turning his head he could see rows of whips, neatly arranged. Below them leaning against the stone walls, were various metal instruments, some straight and some crooked, some long and some shorter, some smooth and some with barbs and hooks. All designed to rend and part the flesh of the human body. On a bench to his left were a jumble of more mundane tools, hammers, awls, pliers, drills, saws of different sizes. Most were clean and shining, as though only recently cleaned. Others were dark-stained.

Although naked, Bogie was not cold. On his right side was a large iron brazier, brimful with glowing charcoal. Resting on the top of it was another assortment of implements. Although he strained his head round, he couldn't quite see exactly what they were, as the tips – the business parts – lay buried beneath the surface of the charcoal. Rags lay ready to wrap around the handles, so that the torturer should not suffer any burnings to the hands while carrying out his duties.

Whatever had gone wrong, it had blown in the biggest possible way. This wasn't the way you usually treated the best friend of a conquering warrior. However, it might be the way you treated the companion of a suspected spy. Any further thoughts along those lines were interrupted by the creaking open of the chamber door, and then the slamming shut of the same door. One pair of feet walked slowly down the steps and clicked along the floor. The men who had carried Bogie down there had left. Looking up, he saw that he was now alone with the Seneschal, Henri Cherneval de Poictiers.

The knight carried a riding-crop in his right hand that he smacked absently against his thigh. Bogie noticed that the crop had metal strands of wire plaited into its ends. The Seneschal came to a halt at the foot of the table and smiled grimly down at him.

'Corporal . . . Hebadiah . . . Fetter.' Punctuating each word by tapping Bogie softly across the unprotected groin. Despite himself he cringed and flinched at each word. Waiting for the blow that he knew was bound to come. Hoping he would be able to faint early on.

De Poictiers poked him a little harder. 'Eyes open. There's a good fellow. Now, Mister Corporal, I will tell you a little tale. Then, when I have finished, you will tell me one. Some fifteen years ago, I hung a family of poachers. Mother, father and a brat of a son. But I spared a young boy. Took him in, cared for him, and sent him off to do the best in the world. He did well. Are you listening?'

As he spoke, de Poictiers had been gently and indifferently using the tip of the crop to flick Bogie across the thighs. Apart from the discomfort, it was an effective way of demonstrating their relative strengths and weaknesses.

'Aye, my lord. I trust this tale of yours will have a merry ending, for I am in need of laughter at present. Unless you have a care with your whip, my lord, I fear that a smile may be all I can raise in the future.'

De Poictiers laughed. 'I like your wit, indeed. I would I had more time to explore it and see how long it would last. But time passes. This boy joined the Galactic Security Service. He began well, I believe. Then we lost track of him. Many thought he would never return, but I, I did not think that. I felt he was bound to me and to this castle in a strange way. I knew that one day he would come back. And, Hebadiah, I was right. Was I not?'

The blow had been expected, but that made the agony none the less. Bogie's body arched up against his bonds, and a harsh gasp of breath whistled through his set teeth.

'My pardon. I was careless there. I would not wish to damage such a splendid member. Doubtless it has pleasured many a maiden and may yet do the same again. If you oblige me with an answer or two.'

Bogart shook the sweat from his eyes. 'First, my lord, a small question of my own. Does it still remain, or was it cut clean off by that blow?'

'It still remains. Would you have proof?'

'No! No, thank you. What is it you wish to know, my lord?'

De Poictiers walked away and came back with a low stool, which he slid gratingly across the floor to a position near Bogie's head. He sat down and comfortably crossed his legs.

'Good. You and I will soon become firm friends. Once this passing unpleasantness has gone, we may laugh over it. I would know where Simon Kennedy Rack is now, what he knows of the Baron's plans, what he intends to do about them? Oh, yes; and what is your name and what part do you play?'

Bogart tried to show no sign of it, but the pain in his groin was nothing compared to the shock of finally knowing, irrevocably, that all was lost. Unless torture was applied with stupidity and senseless brutality, any man would break under it in the end. All he could hope to do was buy Simon a little time.

'My lord de Poictiers. My father was used to say to me that he that didn't fight, but ran away, lived to run away another day. So, working on that assumption, and taking into consideration . . .'

'I wish your name first, since it obviously isn't Hebadiah Fetter. And I do not think you are any sort of fool. Pay me the same compliment, I beg you. We both realise that Rack is trying to get the brushwood men to overthrow this castle. That he will not do because their leader – a brute of an animal, named Morkyn – is in our pay. Ah, that you did not know. I believe he has gone to him because he knows of our plans and how near they are to fruition. I believe you also know them. I believe you play no real part in them, other than to wait here and help if it becomes possible. Now, that has simplified matters. All I need is your name and the answer whether my guesses are correct.' He reached across to the brazier and took out one of the implements. The air shimmered round the white-hot end of it – a thin, corkscrew-like tip – and the Seneschal brought it over and held in front of Bogie's eyes. Even at twenty centimetres or so, the heat made him blink.

'You have an imagination, have you not? Think of the places of your body that I could lay this, or insert the merest part of the tip. No wasting of time, sirrah. None.'

The end of the probe had dulled to a dark red and he placed it back in the fire. Bogie knew it really was all over. When everything else had failed, all that was left was to lie. But, first, a little truth. 'My name is Senior Ensign Eugene Bogart of the Galactic Security Service. And your guesses are a heap of dreck.'

'Dreck?'

'Manure. Ordure. What this castle runs on and is filled with.'

De Poictiers stood up and walked round the table. 'If I'm wrong, brave Ensign Bogart, you might tell me how. And tell me why you are here.'

At that moment the door again creaked open and more steps descended towards them. Dragging steps. Such as a cripple might make.

'Why did you not tell me, Seneschal, that we had two traitors? Two GalSec spies? And that one of them was here in this chamber?' The voice was as gentle as a mild May afternoon. As deadly as a cobra's kiss.

'Because, Lord Magus, I told your father and he did not deem it necessary to tell you. I had believed you to be . . . to be resting.'

The foot dragged across the stones, helped by the rap of the thick, ornately-chased and jewelled cane that the albino always carried. 'I like you least, de Poictiers, when you become a damned mealy-mouthed hypocrite. You knew that I was experimenting with the influences of the magic mushroom. You know I use cocaine and opium. I was not "resting", as you so tastefully put it.'

Bogart had seen the power of the bastard's rages, and saw a chink of hope appear in the armour of despair. He painfully raised his head to look into the drawn face of Magus. 'Why, Master Magus, how pleasant to see your face. Your father has allowed you out of your nursery, has he?'

Magus stepped nearer, his mouth beginning to work. 'You should watch that prattling tongue of yours. Lest you lose it.'

'Brave words to a man bound hand and foot. Helpless and at your mercy. Still, anything less would be a risk for a feeble cripple, hopping through the world like a leprous frog.'

Mescarl's son stepped back as though he had been struck across the face. His red eyes glowed and shifted, his hands went to his throat and tore away the lace, exposing the white skin. A strange and awful noise came from him – half scream, half moan.

De Poictiers hastily stepped in front of him, trying to stop him getting to Bogart. Magus raised his stick and hissed at the Seneschal. 'Stand away from him, or I strike you down.'

'My lord, think what this man knows. Your plans hang so in the balance, that his accomplice may turn a surprise that destroys all. This man may know and he will talk. Think of your father and the plan.'

Slowly, the stick lowered. 'Perhaps. But think not that I lend my mind to this for my father. It is for power that I move. Castle Falcon shall be mine.'

It was time for another jab, while the pot still simmered. 'Don't hold him back on my behalf. I'm a trifle warm and a little fanning wouldn't come amiss. He's only used to tugging wings off flies. He wouldn't be able to hurt a real man.' Again the rage returned. 'Anyway, I doubt he can even lift that stick. He's built more like his mother than his father.'

That was far enough. Still de Poictiers tried to turn him from his purpose, but it was no use. Madness glittered in his face. 'What do you know of my mother?' The words grated slowly through tightened lips.

The blow of mercy. 'I know that your mother hanged herself a week ago. Choked the life out of her own body when she saw the pallid monster she had born, turning into a limping apology for a human being.'

The youth had gone rigid with shock and anger. Clumps of froth hung at the corners of his lips. His left hand clawed at the skin of his face, leaving furrowed trails, the blood startling against the dead-white cheeks. He lurched on his weak leg, and Bogart thought for a moment that he had gone too far and that he was about to fall in a fit. But with a judder of the body, his clenched jaw showing the dreadful effort it took, Magus regained a sort of control.

When he knocked the burly figure of de Poictiers aside, his voice was nearly normal. 'I will kill you, kill you, kill you.' As the stick rose and fell it turned into a chant of triumph.

De Poictiers shouted at him to remember his father. For an instant he paused and looked directly into the Seneschal's eyes, holding them with his own. The older man looked away.

'If need be, I can always replace a father. But there is only one Castle Falcon.' And he turned back to his work.

Seven
Knife And Fire And Candle-light

'So.'

The one word, quietly spoken, hung in the air of the dark hut.

'You followed me. Well, I should have thought of it. You are the daughter of a chief and have been the mistress of one for long enough. So, Master Rack, now you know. You know how whispers of power from a cunning villain like white-faced Magus may make a strong resolve weak and baseless. There is no reason to talk on it, or try and do aught to make me change my thoughts. I am committed to Magus. You will try and tell me that they will betray me. Perhaps. But I tell you this: there is no chance in all this rotten planet that we should win. They hold every ace – power, wealth, men, arms – we hold nothing!'

Simon faced the bigger man and pitched his one throw. 'What of the weapons in the Armoury? What if you held them? Then what might you do?'

There was no reply from Morkyn, but Guenara gasped: 'Not the guns! That is blasphemy. You risk your eternal soul. No man would dare touch a grain of sand from the walls of the Armoury. If he were to look upon one of those foul creations, his sight would wither. His eyeballs would melt in their socket. You are mad!'

Across the room, Morkyn laughed softly. 'I had not thought the Federation had sent a fool.'

The fire flickered for a moment, making the room more light. 'One question, Morkyn. Who says that to know these weapons means death?'

There was the slightest hesitation. 'The priests. And, it is written in the books. Blast you, everyone knows it. What matters who says it? Come now, the people wait for their beds. We must settle this issue before the night is out. I will call a council and you may tell them your new idea. Then I will personally throw you back whence you came.' And he stalked out, the wind of his movement stretching at the tangle of smoke, and winding it about the hut.

Kicking bitterly at the ashes, Simon spoke only to himself, though he intended Guenara to hear him. 'For this I have travelled millions of miles, seen men killed, murdered, suffered, condemned my best friend to a lonely and miserable death. All for a pack of fools. Can't anyone see why the weapons are illegal? Why there is such a taboo on them? Why they are so fearful of anyone getting to them?'

He was interrupted by Guenara. 'Who are "they" Simon? And, why do they do as you say?'

Swinging back on his heel, he reached for her, holding her by the waist and shoulder so that her face was close to his. 'I can say this but once, then we must go out together to face your people. The weapons – bows, swords, spears – that are used here are all simple weapons. Generally, the side with the most *men* will win. And that is always going to be the ruling class. Once you legalise any kind of weapon development, be it gunpowder, cannons, warplanes, atomic grenades – anything – then the small army can have a real chance of beating an infinitely stronger force. One shell could wreck the Castle Falcon. So, who stands to benefit by keeping things as they are? The nobles. Who controls the Church and what books are available? The nobles. Who ensures that even the thought of having a hand-gun is condemned as rankest heresy? Right! Whose reign over these hundreds of years would end overnight if people like you got hold of explosives and used them? That's all there is, Guenara. I swear it's true. But, how can I convince the folk out there? Eh?'

In the darkness the noise increased as Morkyn began to roust the men and women from their huts to attend the meeting of war. Guenara pulled away from him and stood in the open doorway, her figure silhouetted against the blazing fire outside. 'Simon, what you say may be true. It makes a sort of pattern that I can see, and that I think you might make others of us see. But you will need time, and Morkyn will not allow that. They will stone you. What you have said is not better than to blaspheme against the Church. There is only one hope for you. Escape through the back of the hut and take to the woods. I will try and direct them away and you may manage to return to the castle. Give me a few days and I can attempt to talk to others about what you have said here this night. Then, if . . .'

Simon interrupted her. 'Guenara. If I go back to Castle Falcon I will be dead within hours. And there are not days left before the day when Mescarl brings all his threads together. There are scarcely hours.'

A voice thundered from the gathering of wolfsheads in the dark. 'Come, blasphemer and preach your sermon of lies to my people. We are waiting. Or must I drag you out by the ears?'

In the castle the surgeon applied another leech to the neck of the slab of raw meat that had once been Eugene Bogart. Amazingly he lived, though barely. His face was pulped and swollen, livid bruises around the eyes showing where many of the cruellest blows had landed. The lower part of his abdomen was swathed in bandages, blood showing through, obscene against the clean lint. The marks of the cane showed bright on the paler skin. The chest moved slowly, bringing just enough oxygen to the lungs to maintain life. Death sat in the corner of the ill-lit room, wings folded, waiting for his moment.

The lips, puffed and cut, moved. A whisper of words edged out of them to drop into the silence. De Poictiers stepped forward from the black shadows, bending over the injured man. He lowered his head to try and catch the frail sentences. Looking puzzled, he straightened up.

The doctor, a worried-looking man in his late fifties who had seen so many unnecessary injuries and deaths at Castle Falcon, nervously coughed. 'Beg pardon, my lord. But, what did he say? Could you hear it?'

Half-hearing, having forgotten the man's presence, the Seneschal turned. 'What? Oh, I think I must have not heard him properly. I thought he said: "For the love of God, Montresor." Whatever that means. Odd.'

The noise was subdued but, none-the-less, menacing. The mob was opposed to him, simply because he wore the hated livery of Baron Mescarl. The word had gone round that he was an agent of a police force of some kind that was opposed to Baron Mescarl and that he had come to free them. But Morkyn had quickly put the word about that Simon was, in fact, a black magician who threatened the roots of their beliefs.

So, it was confusion. A sullen, bitter confusion. Their hopes had been briefly raised, only to be quickly dashed. Many secretly thought that things would never change. That they would always be wolfsheads, hunted by soldiers, every bondsman's hand against them. Eating acorns and moss, drinking stagnant water, living in stinking hovels, babies dying before their time. Dry throats in summer and cracked hands in winter.

Light had come into their darkness and had then been switched off. Now they would turn on the intruder. Since he could never persuade them in that mood, and he could not fight them all, he had but one choice.

'Morkyn!' he shouted as he burst out of the blackness of the hut, leaving Guenara behind him. 'I say that you are a coward. A damned coward. A yellow bitch that fawns secretly at the boots of the skull-faced son of black Mescarl. Who licks the mud from his path and then begs for a sweetmeat as a reward for his loyal service.'

There was no point in going further. Shouts from the surrounding crowd drowned his voice. Some cried for him to be silenced, while others yelled for combat and for Morkyn to slay him. A few stood mute and puzzled. Rack did not look the sort of man who wished to die so bloodily.

By waving his hands around and banging a few heads together, Morkyn managed a sort of silence. The sort of quiet when everyone keeps breath ready to break it. An uneasy quiet.

'I can admire bravery in a man, but not this sort of madness. You think to convince people of your lies by this foolishness. What will you gain by it?'

'I would have these folk know the sort of man who leads them. A base traitor, who has sold them out to Mescarl. A man who has taken their dreams and crushed them in his vile hands. A man, Morkyn, that I will destroy for them.'

Again the bedlam rose about him and it was difficult to make himself heard. 'Listen to me! I say that Morkyn is a traitor. I will prove it on my body by fighting and killing him. I loathe slaughter, but I would have no more feeling for this arrant renegade than I would for stepping on some poisonous spider. By your own rules, if I win against him, I will be your leader. And I will lead you against the pile of the Castle Falcon. Together we will bring it low, and hang its vile master from his own battlements. But, first . . .'

'First, you must slay me. Aye, quiet. Quiet!! Simon has right on his side. It will avail him little when we do battle. But if he should defeat me, he will be your leader and you must follow him and do his bidding. If I am the man he claims in his shrill accusations, then God will surely be on his side. Mayhap he will lift me over his head and fling me around Standon spire.'

Once the laughter had died down, everyone set to with a will to prepare for the combat. The outlaws made a rough ring around the fire in the centre of their huts. Many held lights so the area was well-lit. More wood was placed on the fire and the earth was trampled flatter. Both men stripped to their breeches; Simon discarded his boots, but Morkyn chose to keep his on. Morkyn was even more impressive peeled for action – his chest like a wall of stone covered in wiry, tangled hair – his muscles bounding under the skin. By the side of the outlaw, Simon looked a slender youth.

Guenara came to him as they readied themselves. 'Watch for him. He is strong and fast. He can use both hands with equal ease and he will not hesitate to use foul means to win. Also I think he may have a knife hidden at the front of his breeches.'

'Why do you tell me this Guenara?'

She paused before replying. 'Because, I think you may be right in what you say. I have lived all my life, hunted and running. Wherever I walk, I must keep my head aslant, to watch lest I am followed. I know that I will not live for long for things are worse and we are harried over-much. Perhaps I can live a little as I would wish if you are right.'

Wat then called Simon and Morkyn together and the words were ended. The rules of combat were short and simple. There were none. They should fight until one or the other was defeated and admitted his wrong. Or, as was more usual, until one was dead. Weapons were not to be used. As Wat stepped back, ready to give the signal to begin, Morkyn muttered at Simon: 'Once you are dead, I will use that slut for my own pleasure. Then I will strangle her. In two days, my lord will have won his game. And I will rule these lands. And you, Simon, will lie rotting on our midden, with children playing over your corpse and flies feasting on your eyes.'

Wat had reached the security of the ring of watchers and held his hand high. He dropped it.

Simon immediately began to back away, sizing up the bigger man. Morkyn walked round after him, hands outstretched for the chance to tear him. He mocked the speed of Simon's retreat and Simon ignored him. But as he edged past where he knew Wat was, a large rock was thrown from the crowd, hitting painfully below the right shoulder. He staggered forward and Morkyn was on him.

One hand, like a vice, seized his left fore-arm, while the other grappled for his ribs. Instead of trying to pull away, Simon dived instantly inside the outlaw's grasp, his head coming up sharply under his chin, knocking his head back. Blood ran from Morkyn's cut lip and the crowd shrieked.

Again they shuffled across the rough arena. Morkyn leaped at Simon, arms ready to crush, but Simon was no longer there. As he lumbered past him, Simon delivered a cracking cut at the top of the forearm. Morkyn roared with the unexpected pain and pulled back, rubbing the numb arm.

Simon smiled. He knew now he could win. The man was big and immensely strong, but he was slow. Slow in thought and slow in action.

He advanced warily, balanced on the balls of his feet,

while Morkyn began to give ground. They were close to the fire when Morkyn made his try. His hand crept down the front of his breeches and whipped out holding a stubby-bladed knife.

There was a low cry of disapproval from his followers and Simon didn't miss the chance. 'So Morkyn, you are a traitor in everything you do. Treacherous bastard!'

At least Morkyn knew how to fight with a knife. He came forward again, his blade held low in his right hand, point upwards, weaving it in a web of hypnotic death. Simon pretended fear and ran back, slipping in the loose sand. The watchers gasped and he heard, or thought he heard, a cry from Guenara. He got to his feet just in time to avoid a rush. In his hand, clasped tight, was dust. Simon Rack rarely fell accidentally!

He carefully manoeuvred his man until his back was to the blazing fire. Then he darted in; the knife hissed at him, but the sand was thrown at Morkyn's face. Instinctively, both his hands went up to try and save his eyes from the burning of the grit. For a moment the knife was waving uselessly at shoulder height.

Now! Straighten and pivot on the left foot. Strike out and up with the right foot, hit him clearly in the groin. Padding of some kind. Still hard enough to double him up. Knife next. Under the arm, hit the triceps. Edge of the hand biting into the muscle, bruising the bone. Knife in the dirt. Kick it out of the way with the right foot. He's straightening up. Jab at his guts. Board of muscle but not that strong. Fingers dig in. Upwards, under the sternum. Can kill but not an ox like Morkyn. Panting. God, he's strong!

A watcher who knew nothing of fighting skills would still have thought the odds were on the stronger man. Most of the brushwood folk who watched in the flickering light knew much of fighting, and they had become quiet.

Simon slipped in like a striking cobra, and slapped Morkyn contemptuously across the cheek. 'Well, traitor. How think you the battle goes? Your Lord Magus will not aid you now. Eh!'

Morkyn made no answer. His chest heaved and sweat ran off his face. Back to the fire, he loomed big. But Simon knew it was over. It was just a matter of waiting for the way to show.

He dropped his hands to rub his groin. Up. Both feet way off the ground, lashing at the unprotected face. Teeth snapped and splintered and the nose was crushed inwards; fragments of bone from the ruined nose were driven up and into the front part of the brain. It was a terrible blow.

Giving a loud cry, Morkyn toppled backwards like a hewn pine, fingers trying to hold his face together, the last conscious efforts of his dying brain.

He rolled face down into the fire, scattering ashes and glowing branches. Flames licked about his head and shoulders, ate up his beard and hair, nibbled at the skin of his face. Muffled by the burning charçoal that enveloped his mouth, agonised screams and animal moans came from the dying man. His hands jerked convulsively, clawing at the fire, trying helplessly to lever his body out of the fire.

Simon rose to his feet, wiped his hands across his face, and looked for the knife. It lay close to the fire, its blade reflecting the burst of sparks as death came slowly to Morkyn the outlaw. Morkyn the traitor.

Simon picked up the knife and dragged the twitching body out of the fire by its feet. The hair was all gone from the blackened skull and it was difficult to pull back the head to cut the throat and end the suffering. He managed to lever his hand under the charred chin, and tug back the head. Most of the face was scorched and the eyelids quite burned through.

When the edge of the knife slid through the right carotid artery, the jet of blood gushed into the fire, steaming and filling the clearing with the stench of roasting. As the flow weakened, the heart ceased to pump and the brain stopped functioning. Simon laid the corpse on the earth and stood up.

'Now I am your leader. By your own rules I am your leader. If any man question that, let him stand out now. Wat? No? You have seen what I can do. It's too late now for any discussion or planning. Go to your beds. Think over what you have seen. I swear to you, as an officer of the Galactic Security Service, a representative of the Federation, that this man was a traitor to you. On the morrow, after we have all broken our fasts, I will tell you of my plans. To many they will seem blasphemy. But they are not. Now go to your huts and sleep.'

Talking quietly, one to another, the people began to drift into the outer dark. Simon called out and checked them.

'Wat! You and I have a score between us. I will hold no grudge with a man who I wish to fight on my side. I will see it settled if you will take this offal out and bury it where it will not offend the nostrils of honest folk. Then our score will be level. What say you?'

Wat ran forward so hastily that he stumbled and nearly fell. 'Aye, Simon. Gladly. I meant nothing by it. I believed Morkyn. I am sorry for spitting.'

Simon reached out with the hand holding the knife, so that the point pricked Wat's cheek. 'And the stone, Wat. Are you also sorry for that?'

The man paled. 'Oh, the stone. Aye, Simon. For that too.'

'Now go, Wat, and bury him well. Then in the morrow we will talk of the living.'

He looked round the arena, deserted, but for one woman. In front of the hut that had been Morkyn's, Guenera stood waiting. Simon walked towards her, feeling the tiredness and tension dragging at his feet.

'You did well, my lord.' She curtsied to him. 'Where will you sleep, my lord?'

'In the hut of the chief; where else would I sleep?'

'Then I will sleep with you. No, I am decided. For am I not the mistress of the chief? Where else should I sleep?'

Later that night, all passion spent, his tiredness eased by Guenara's love, Simon drifted into a quiet sleep. Outside, the fire had died down, and the hut was dark and silent. Beside him, the woman lay in sleep, her hair framing the sun-browned face. His head lay across her naked breast, the nipple brushing his lips as she moved in a dream.

Tomorrow would be a day for planning. The day after that a time for action.

Simon's last waking thought was of Bogart, wondering how he had met his death. Hoping it had not been slow.

Eight
In My End Is My Beginning

Twenty-four hours had passed. Morkyn lay quietly rotting in a forest grave. Bogart had still not recovered consciousness and lay in a truckle bed in the castle. Occasionally he would shake his head and murmur. De Poictiers spent what time he could spare in the sick-room, waiting for some clue in the ramblings that would reveal any danger to his master's plans. In two day's time the plans would be beyond any hindrance. Then what remained of Bogart would be taken to the gallows on the west wall of the inner bailey. His arms and legs would be strapped, and he would be lowered into space, there to swing and pivot until the flesh withered away, the tendons parted, and what was left would drop, like a bunch of dried twigs, to the cobbles thirty metres below.

Mescarl and the visiting lords and ladies confined their pleasures to the castle, lest a sneak attack deplete their numbers further. There were mock tourneys, and Mescarl played a challenge match of chess, with players culled from the dungeons. His opponent, Malan, was mated in eighteen moves, and personally slew his own queen as a token of his defeat.

Magus had not been seen all that day, after the beating he had given to Bogart. His chamber door remained firmly locked, and food and drink left outside was not touched. The casement windows stayed veiled with black velvet. A servant, bolder than the rest, crept up and placed his ear to the door, reporting he heard only chanting and the hollow beating of a slack-skinned drum. Other serfs trembled and doubted not his words when he told them that he had not only heard the piping voice of the albino lordling. Though all knew the rooms were deserted but for Magus, the servant swore he heard another voice speaking. A deep voice, speaking a strange tongue, with tones like a bubbling echo, coming through thick liquid at a great distance.

Miles away, in the woods, deep buried, Simon had spent the day taking small numbers of the brushwood folk into the hut, and slowly and gently trying to educate them for the part he was asking them to play on the morrow. He knew well what he was trying. Persuading Colonel Stacey to stand on his own desk and urinate all over the GalSec regulations would be an easy task by comparison.

Guenara was a pillar of strength beside him, for she knew all the people and their ways. She had come to see that what Simon said made sense, and that it might bring hope where there had been none. With some she argued, some she joked with, some she threatened. Some would not ever be able to alter their ingrained beliefs. Some were partly convinced. Some, the more intelligent, saw the argument and were with them.

He had talked to them all after, the believers and the doubters. He had taken his sword and drawn a line in the centre of the arena. 'Tomorrow I will ride against Castle Falcon and I will bring down the power of Baron Mescarl or I will leave my bones to whiten here on the earth of Sol Three. Any man who will fight with me, cross over this line and stand at my shoulder. If none come, I swear to ride alone. Decide.'

For a moment there was no movement. Old habits die hard and no man wishes to give up his life, however hard it may be, for a doubtful cause against odds that centuries of conditioning told him were insurmountable. There was a flurry in the crowd and Guenara burst out and strode across to stand by him.

'So, my love, it will be you and I alone. These cowardly curs will sleep at their firesides and bring more brats into the world who will live in this filth and die before they have begun to live.' She turned to the shame-faced crowd. 'You fools. You have heard what Simon has said. Once Mescarl's plan is safe, think you he will permit a nest of waspish outlaws – though they all be cowards – in his demesne? You know now why we have been safe for so long. In two days we will be as good as dead. Why wait for that? Let us at least find a way of dying that will not shame us.'

Wat was one of the first to come to them, followed by others in ones and twos. Women pushed their men forward, while some of the older girls also came out. Finally, only the very young, the older women, and a couple of crippled and aged men were left beyond the line.

Evening nudged the day aside and threw long shadows between the huts. Simon, following Guenara's advice, appointed four lieutenants, rejected some of the girls and a few of the older men and boys. He was left with a fighting force of forty-eight men and twelve women. With that pocket army, he intended to storm the strongest fortress in all of Sol Three and defeat a garrison of trained soldiers numbering well over two hundred, plus the guards of the visiting nobles.

After careful and detailed planning sessions, Simon sent his lieutenants away to take their own units through the strategy until each man was word-perfect in the part he would play in the attack. There was no more he could do.

The hut was empty, but for Guenara and himself. She cut thick hunks of wholemeal bread, coarse-grained, and handed them to him with a bowl of harsh-tasting goat's milk cheese. He had not found time to eat during the day and he wolfed it down. A leather cup of ale followed to smooth out some of the sandy crevices in his throat. While he lay back on the skins, Guenara closed the curtain that shielded the front entrance and came to him.

Kneeling by him, she began to unlace him from his clothes. 'Do you think we have a chance?'

Simon forced himself to stay awake. 'If they see us too soon their arbalastiers will cut us down like a herd of deer. If we can get close, get to the Armoury, then we might have a chance.'

Although she caressed him with all her skill, sleep proved a more successful enchantress for Simon Rack than Guenara. She covered him with skins and, a little sadly, lay beside him. By tomorrow night she would be dead or one of the rebels who had toppled a ruling class that had owned men's lives for hundreds of years. Either way, she would be free.

The peasants began arriving early at Castle Falcon. With the numbers of extra visitors there, the outer bailey was packed soon after sun-up with an unusually large crowd of local people selling their wares. In case of trouble, de Poictiers had doubled the guards that stood at intervals around the inner walls of the bailey and had also posted extra men at the key position of the postern gate. The Armoury had been defended with extra men-at-arms ever since the first of the conspiring nobles had arrived.

De Poictiers had intended to watch the outer gates himself, to try and spot any familiar faces from the wolfsheads, particularly one Simon Rack. But duties concerning the key movements of pheronium from quarry to secret processing plant had taken him away for a couple of hours in the morning.

The market ran as usual, despite the larger numbers. Simon deliberately kept back his attack until the guards had become casual in their watching. Had relaxed, thinking there was to be no trouble.

His plan was simple. The first move would be struck by the women, under Guenara. They were to station themselves near to one of the men-at-arms, with keen-edged knives ready under their cloaks. One party of men, under the command of a tough ex-soldier called Ralph, was to stand by with short hunting bows and arrows hidden among the produce they had brought. Their task was to help the women if there was trouble and then try and check any attacks by archers within the castle walls who might fire at the attackers from the safety of casements or embrasures.

Twenty more, under Wat, were to position themselves as near as possible to the postern gate without arousing suspicion. As soon as the women made their move, they were to rush the gate and hold it at all costs.

The remaining dozen – the best men that Guenara had been able to recommend – stuck close to Simon and were to attempt the impossible task of taking the impregnable Armoury. They had wicks wound about their waists and their barrels of vegetables concealed water bags full of inflammable cooking oil.

The midday bell had sounded in the belfry above the Well Tower. Thirty more minutes and the guard would be changed. One hour more and the market would be closed. Simon, hooded and cloaked, peered across the courtyard to where Guenara was haggling with an elderly woman about the price of her beans. She caught his glance, ignoring the old woman's plaint about overcharging. He nodded sharply, and she smiled back at him.

He had been briefly tempted by the idea of the grand

gesture. The noble cry for freedom and liberty. But the longer secrecy could be kept, the better for all. Each second saved could mean the life of one of his small party. Now she had his signal, Guenara would pass it on in the way they had agreed. Wat and Ralph would be listening for it and would act.

'Why, you insulting old harridan! May the flesh rot on my bones if I sell rotten food! You can't come here saying that about honest folk. I'll have the law on you. I'll go right to the Lord himself. See if Baron Mescarl thinks I'm a felon!'

Despite the tension, Simon could not help smiling. It had been agreed that she would stage a row, and that the password should be the name of Mescarl. The look on the face of the woman who had been haggling with her showed a mixture of amazement and embarrassment at the sudden and noisy outburst.

If she could have seen the results of the shout, she would have been a hundred times more amazed. Round the walls of the outer bailey, soldiers lounged back, enjoying the sun, thinking of the food and drink that waited for them in less than half an hour. What happened to young Godfric was typical of what happened to them all.

Godfric was hardly even awake. His mail chafed at his neck and his armpits, while sweat trickled down his chest. His groin itched, but there was no way he could get at it to scratch. Not for another half hour. The market was more crowded than usual, and noisier. What was that loudmouthed slut shouting about? Pray God there wasn't going to be any trouble! Not just before he went off duty. No, it seemed to be quietening down. Another woman coming over to him. Not one of the girls from the dello touting for trade! What did she say?

'Speak up, lovely. What?'

The soldier bent his head to the level of the girl's mouth.

The big arteries in the throat are clearly visible as they pulse with the beats of the heart pushing the blood to and from the brain. The previous evening all the women had been instructed by Guenara in where and how to strike. The whetstone had whirled and sparked far into the night as an edge was put on every knife. Beth, the girl who was about to kill Godfric, was trembling as she struck, but the blow was hard enough and accurate. The point of the knife dug in just behind the jugular and she pulled it forward as she had been told.

Blood sprayed into her eyes and she was nearly sick, but it was done. The soldier didn't make a sound, though his eyes opened very wide with surprise. Death closed down his mind so fast that he never had a chance to realise what had happened. His last thought was regret that something had stung him sharply on the neck, just as a pretty girl was going to tell him something interesting.

Although few of the peasants realised it at first, every man-at-arms in the outer bailey was dead within fifteen seconds. Only one managed a shout and he was cut down by one of Ralph's party standing nearby. But cries from all around revealed that some had seen the killings. Shouts and screams multiplied geometrically until the courtyard was a bedlam. Men and women fought each other as they tried to get out of the castle. Vegetables rolled and bounced on the cobbles and eggs smashed and mingled with the streams of blood from the dead men. Chickens fluttered and squawked and a pig rushed around, a string dangling from its rear leg.

Near the postern Wat's group moved speedily into action as soon as they heard the word. They found a larger number of soldiers there than they had expected but surprise was on their side and their losses were small. Within a minute the guardhouse was a shambles with dead men lying across the floor. Wat ordered the bodies thrown into the outer bailey to clear the space for fighting. The door to the outside was left open, while the inner door was closed and barred.

Four of the men with bows pounded up the spiral staircase to the chamber above the guardroom to command a view of the inner courtyard. A sergeant who had been sleeping in the room was sufficiently awakened by the noise below to sell his life at a cost, by killing one of the bowmen and wounding two of the others. But the postern was secured.

The guards on the outer gate shut the portcullis as soon as they realised something was wrong, but by then most of the peasants were out and running as fast as their legs would take them.

The outer bailey was cleared and rested in Simon's hands. Ralph's men, backed by the women, attacked the outer gateway, taking advantage of the panic there. In fact, it held for nearly ten minutes, and half the attackers gave their lives for it. But, once it had fallen, the portcullis could be raised and the main entrance held open. Surviving bowmen spread thinly out around the moat and waited out of castle bow-shot for the final part of the plan.

Simon waited only a few minutes to see if the first stages were safely under way, then led his group to the Black Tower housing the Armoury of forbidden weapons.

Overhead, the tocsin clanged out a warning to the defenders of the castle that the unbelievable was happening. Castle Falcon had been infiltrated by a small band of determined fighters. Amazingly, within less than two minutes, the whole outer half of the fortress was under the control of the outlaws. But it was a tenuous hold, and would only last as long as the postern could be kept. Already men were mustering in the inner bailey, ready to storm it.

So far, thought Simon, remembering the story of Sarah

in the Red Mouse – years ago it seemed – so good. Casualties were no worse than he'd feared. Now it was his turn.

The Black Tower lay to the left of the courtyard as one entered the castle. It was hewn granite, about one hundred feet high. The ground floor was purely for the soldiers who defended the tower for twenty-four hours every day of the year. The weapons were kept on the top floors.

Two men stood outside the main door and they died immediately, their chests feathered with arrows. The heavy door was rushed and thrown back before the men inside were aware of the threat. A brief bloody hacking followed in the main room before it was cleared. But reinforcements were at hand and the fighting became savage and desperate.

Simon led the attack, sword singing in his hand. He cut and parried furiously, while men behind him secured one of the side rooms that Bogart had picked as being suitable for beginning the fire. Mattresses stored there were shredded and slashed, the straw being soaked in the heavy oil.

Drinking water from the copper-bound butt near the door was splashed on more of the mattresses. All this while men fought and died for time. A cry from behind him told Simon that enough time had been bought and he retreated slowly.

He found Guenara at his elbow, swinging a long-handled axe. Although they were falling back, the defenders suspected a trap and didn't follow them. In the side room flint and stones were struck together and a box of carefully shielded tinder ignited. The oil-soaked straw was set alight and a great blaze lit up the ground floor. There were cries of alarm from the soldiers and a sally was attempted. But the angles of walls and stairs made it difficult for them to come to grips with their numerically inferior enemies and the sally was repulsed.

The one thing that the planners of the castle had not

foreseen was that defenders might want to fight their way out rather than hold off attackers, so even the turns of the spiral stairs made it hard for a swordsman to give a good account of himself.

The wooden floors were age-old and dry as dust. Flames licked along them and leaped up doors. Tables sprouted tongues of flame and wall-hangings exploded into instant ash. Simon yelled for the wet mattresses to be used before the whole tower erupted into fire. If the burning were not quickly checked, the plan would be lost along with the banned guns.

The sodden cotton bags of straw were heaved on top of the blazing oil and instantly belched out thick, choking smoke. Simon led his men near to the main doorway, where the air was purer. The fumes were so heavy that it was impossible to see a metre in front of one's eyes and they could already hear coughing and cursing from the defenders as the grey-white smoke billowed around them.

To appreciate the genius of the plan for taking the Armoury you need to see what Bogart's military experience had spotted on that brief reconnaissance days earlier. Well-built though the Black Tower was it contained two fundamental flaws. Both of which had been skilfully exploited by the attackers. First, the main door was vulnerable to a surprise attack. Secondly, the whole building was designed in a series of segments, each a few feet higher than the other, circling upwards round a large central stairway. Like a number of wood and stone triangles, each overlapping on the other, wheeling about the centre.

What that created was a huge chimney that would direct any smoke from the ground floor cycloning furiously towards the top floors. And there was no way of cutting it off.

'Can we do nothing now, my lord?' asked Guenara, as they waited in the doorway.

'No. The outer gate is ours, Wat holds the middle gate. All we can do is let the smoke fill this tower.'

Already smoke gushed from every embrasure and window in the forbidding fortress. Every now and again, a head would appear at an opening, gasping for breath, or crying for help. None of Mescarl's men had yet asked for quarter. They knew the price that would be paid by any who surrendered once the Baron or de Poictiers reasserted order. And, against a handful of raggle-taggle wolfsheads that surely wouldn't take long.

In the postern tower things were becoming warm. The attackers had a ram out and were pounding on the sturdy door. In the rooms above, the surviving archers poured a steady stream of death into the inner bailey, and the cobbles were splattered with blood and dotted with grotesquely flung bodies.

Behind a mantelet, the Seneschal urged his men on to greater efforts. The pillar of smoke that writhed above the Black Tower told its own tale. A tale that meant a warning. De Poictiers now knew enough of Simon, and remembered more, to make his fists tense with worry. Would he dare to take the Armoury? And, if he did, would he . . .? The thought was too appalling, and he put it away from him and cursed the men with the battering-ram.

Looking back on it later, the next quarter of an hour was a blur of action. Of death and violence. Of smoke and dirt. Simon found he could remember only fleeting impressions of events – some trivial and some vital.

There was the moment when the first defender of the Black Tower found he could no longer stand the suffocating reek and leaped silently to smash his body to shreds on the iron cobbles thirty metres below. He struck with such a force that Simon, standing a distance away, was splashed by the man's brains as his head split like an earthenware jar.

Others followed, spinning earthwards like a cluster of autumn leaves. Simon grouped the survivors of his band ready for the final desperate attack that he guessed would not be long in coming as desperation seized the defenders. Because of a lack of planned charge by the defenders, they were able to deal easily with the straggling thread of coughing, choking soldiers, red of eye as they stumbled towards the air and light of the bailey.

Guenara, hacking them behind the knees with her axe, cutting through the unprotected tendons, then pulping their heads as they fell helplessly. And laughing as she did it. Her long hair becoming matted with gouts of blood.

Closing the door on the fire and cutting it off to a trickle of thin smoke. Killing the few men who had held out on the top floors. Men weakened by a lack of air. Everything dusted with soot and sticky to the touch of a sweating hand.

Then the gallery with the earlier explosive weapons. Being alone as the others – despite their courage – could not cross the taboo barrier. Guenara mocking them and breaking the glass of a display, waving a small hand-gun about. Pointing it at Simon, moving it when she saw the look on his face. The others, gaining courage from her, laughing together as they seized weapons.

Shouting at them to leave them alone. Guns of that age would be totally unreliable, the charges long rotted into useless powder. On the next floor he found what he had been hoping for. A large display case of irradiant twisters, barely a hundred years old. If the harcon charges were still active and functioning, they would be capable of killing any man in extreme agony by exploding their abdominal cells. The victim would be convulsed with a hideous rictus of pain – thus giving the weapons their nickname of twisters.

He turned the dial up to eleven-point-eight – maximum

for that particular model – and looked around for a way of testing it. It would have been convenient if there had been one soldier left behind and overlooked who would charge suicidally at Simon, only to be cut down by the gun.

Life isn't that considerate and Simon had to turn the dial full down and risk a shot at his own stomach. He got the vibration he hoped for and a stab of severe nausea. They worked!

Shouting above the noise of the pealing bell and the screams and yells from outside the tower, Simon managed to give them the most elementary weapon training – so sparse that it would have made the last few hairs tumble from the shining pate of old Under-officer Newman, his GalSec instructor.

He also found a couple of grenade launchers with a dozen rounds of ammunition. The armoury had fallen barely in time.

Even as the attackers were clattering down the stone stairs, they met one of Wat's postern party, bleeding heavily from cuts to face and left shoulder. The attack on them from the inner bailey had nearly broken through.

Dashing over floors slick with spilled blood into the slaughterhouse of the guard-room where only three men stood to thrust through the splintered timbers of the oak door. One falling with a pike-head torn off between the ribs, back into Simon's arms. Blood frothing up from punctured lungs. Wat. Face contorted with the agony of dying, seeing the gun in Simon's hand. Touching it, as though it were a holy relic of a blessed saint. Smiling. Dying.

A round dozen of the wolfsheads still on their feet, none without a wound. Guenara slashed in the thigh, dress falling open at the cut. Himself with a sword cut high on the right arm, where a parry had missed. Another dark stain of red under the left arm where an arrow had pinked him.

Each of them with a forbidden weapon in his or her hand, faces streaked with smoke. Facing three-quarters of Castle Falcon's Forces, under the personal leadership of the experienced Seneschal. About to crush the last of the rebels and hang any that lived as an example of what happened to any who dared stand against rightful authority.

Remembering the next moments, Simon always skipped them as quickly as could be. Time was so tight as they clustered in that postern room that there was no chance of a parley, no hope of merely stunning the men-at-arms. It had to be death.

One or two of the guns failed to activate, but the rest cut swathes through the soldiers. Dozens fell on the spot, their bodies thrashing with the awful pain, biting through their own tongues. None hit by the twisters lived. Their stomachs literally exploded, webs of intestine instantly becoming crystalline.

The ram dropping, men running back. Dying until the stones of the inner bailey were darkened with writhing bodies. Soon still with the weight of corpses. Simon stopping firing, others around doing the same. Guenara weeping at the horror of mass death. A sudden shocking silence.

Taking two of the grenades and exploding them as harmlessly as he could against opposite walls, by the Well Tower and by the Queen's Tower, blowing fragments of stone high in the air, tearing at the fabric of the castle. A stunned group of survivors, huddled at the base of the Falcon Tower, more near the mantelet where de Poictiers still crouched.

Shouting for their surrender, speaking direct to the Seneschal. Pleading for an end to death. De Poictiers walking forward alone, sword in hand. Pausing when twenty paces from them. Snapping his sword across his knees and then ordering his men to lay down their arms. Saying nothing.

The screams from the apartments of Baron Mescarl, a trembling of the window hangings of Magus's room. Nobles leaning from casements and cursing their own men for cowards.

Each one of Simon's group taking prisoners to the dungeons. The castle theirs. Resistance quelled as much by the apocalyptic sight of the long-forbidden weapons as by the dreadful effect they had. Keeping clear of the Falcon Tower, leaving it till last. Sealing it up with four men with twisters.

An hour and all was safe. The final clearing remained. Asking about Bogart; when he'd died. That he had been taken to the Falcon Tower. Alive!

The gates opened, and all the rest of the outlaws in both baileys and on the battlements.

Having whittled away all of the roots and the trunk of the old, old tree, there remained only the matter of lopping off the topmost branches.

Cupping his hands to his mouth, Simon stood close to the walls of Falcon Tower and shouted his message. 'My name is Commander Simon Rack – an officer of the Galactic Security Service of the Federation, under whose jurisdiction this planet is. I have ample evidence that the fundamental rules of the Federation have been flagrantly breached. Also that there is a wide-reaching conspiracy involving every noble now present in this castle to engage the entire Federation by withholding sufficient of pheronium until a monstrous ransom had been exacted.'

He calmly stepped aside as a large mahogany chair smashed through the glass of one of the windows above him and broke on the cobbles where he had been standing.

'To kill an officer of the Galactic Security Service while on active duty is a capital offence. Any of you who wish to surrender to Federation justice will come, unarmed, to this courtyard within five minutes. After the expiry of that time I will come in with my followers and clean out this stinking nest of rats. And opposition will be suppressed.'

Dribbling out in small numbers, most of the lords and ladies gave themselves up, knowing they faced a lengthy period of medical re-education in one of the Federation's penal colonies. For most that was preferable to certain death. All of their mercenary guards also gave themselves up, knowing they faced much less severe sentences. Simon picked out a dozen or so of the top men from amongst them and made them responsible for security in the over-crowded prison quarters. Knowing well where their best chances lay, they accepted eagerly.

Once the five minutes were up, Simon gave one last warning. 'Remember what I said about killing an officer of the Federation. If my number two, Ensign Bogart still lives, I will summarily execute any man who lays a hand on him.'

Amongst those who had not yet surrendered were Mescarl, Magus and Lord Malan. Quick words with the mercenaries indicated that the Falcon Tower now held a scant dozen souls.

Guenara at his side, his twister in his hand, Simon led his raiding party into the luxurious quarters of the masters of Sol Three. The ground floor and the first floor revealed nothing more menacing than the bodies lying together on a bed of a lord and lady, richly-clothed. From the scent of almonds on their breaths, it was clear that they had chosen to end their own lives together rather than face humiliation and a long separation.

Five more bodies lay on the next floor. Again a family. Three young children butchered with a sword, a wife with her head half-severed and the husband with his own throat cut. The sword lay near his hand where it had dropped after he had completed his gory work.

A voice floated down to them from the floor above. The

voice of Malan. 'Commander. I note your words about how wicked it is to kill one of you GalSec wretches. But I fear I am too deep in blood for one more death to lie more heavily on me than another. So, since it seems that all is left to me is revenge, you will forgive me if I indulge a little in that admitted pettiness. In my hand I have a knife and at the point of that knife is your Ensign.'

'Alive?'

'Amazingly so. Yes. Amazingly, if you were to see what Lord Magus had done to him in one of his tiresomely childish rages.'

While he spoke, Simon began to creep soundlessly up the winding staircase. Hoping the man would carry on with his vicious prattle. But he was too late.

'I do not hear you, Commander, but I would hazard a guess that you are more than half-way up the stairs to me by now. Listen, the sound you will hear will be the life-blood – what little is left of it – splashing out of your comrade. Are you . . . Aaaaagh!'

Simon took the rest of the steps at full run and burst in through the half-open door of the chamber. The sound of the scuffle and Malan's sudden strangled scream were immediately explained. The noble was on his knees in the straw, tugging purple-faced at a pair of legs that were wrapped firmly around his neck, crushing his white lace ruff. The legs belonged to a bizarre, naked apparition. It was a stocky figure of a man, his genitals almost obscured by swelling and bruising. His chest and torso were also badly marked while his face was hidden under a huge gag of torn cotton. Above the cotton an eye peered hopefully at Simon, the other eye being closed and blue-black. The arms were stretched up and chained to rings near the ceiling. It was Bogart.

Simon smashed the lord across the head with the pommel of the sword he still carried in his left hand and quickly hacked through the fetters at their joining links. Bogart promptly collapsed in the straw, his arms useless from the strain they had been under. Simon eased off the gag and sat him up.

Bogart rolled his swollen lips, his tongue working to bring a little moisture. 'Sweet God, you took your time, Simon. I thought yon ferret would have stuck me like an insect with a pin before you arrived.' He then noticed Guenara standing in the doorway with a twister in her hand, her face covered in soot and blood. 'Madam, I trust you'll forgive me for the informality of my attire. Not really the way to receive a lady, I know. Is all well, Simon?'

Unable to stop grinning with the pleasure of finding Bogart alive – if not exactly well – Simon quickly filled him in on what had happened. Bogart interrupted him: 'Magus. I think he's the real evil here. Worse than Mescarl. He did most of this to me. His room is on this floor.'

His followers pressing about him, Simon rose to go after the biggest fish in the pool. He detailed two men to remain behind and look after Bogart. Pausing in the doorway, he turned to ask one question. 'Was it too bad? Really?'

Bogie tried a grin that nearly slipped clean off his face with the pain. 'Tell you all later. Not that bad. Most of the time I spent just hanging around.' And he winked with his good eye.

A wave and Simon was gone. There was nobody on that floor, but they found Magus's suite of rooms securely locked. They hammered ineffectively on the brass panels and pressed their ears to try and catch a sound. There was only a chill and total quiet. The landing outside the rooms smelled of myrrh and was colder than one might have expected.

'Come. We will return to the brat when we have dealt with his father. Two of you stay here. Be on your guard against treachery from chalk-face.'

So Simon, Guenara and two others climbed to the topmost floor of Falcon Tower, which was at the highest level of all the floors of Castle Falcon.

It was empty!

Mescarl had escaped them. None of the rooms had an occupant. In a fury Simon ripped down every tapestry and overturned every piece of furniture. He looked wildly in every corner, rapped the walls and stamped on the floors. There was not the least sign of the Baron.

Closing his eyes and sitting down suddenly on one of the beds, Simon gathered all his mental strength together and calmed himself. It would be absurd to fail now. He was here, therefore Mescarl *must* be here. Somewhere. He was not in the rooms. He was not behind the walls anywhere. He was not below the floors. Therefore . . . Simple.

The ceilings were heavily ornamented and patterned. The only ones in the castle to be so painted. Once he was clear what he sought, it took moments for Simon to spot the panel in the bedroom, concealed by a rectangular design of purple and black.

Aided by the men, he piled up tables and chairs until he could probe the crack with the point of his sword. A catch snapped back and he was able to push up the trap-door and scramble into the beams and rafters of the roof. There was a silk ladder tangled up in the loft and he threw it down for his return.

To his surprise it tightened immediately as someone began to climb. He peered back down through the trap and saw the figure of Guenara. Even as she climbed he tried to persuade her to stay down. It would have been as easy to check the stars in their courses. Panting hard, she pulled herself up and smiled at him.

'Don't chide me, my lord. Know you not that I have the gift of seeing. I walked last night in the forest and traced the pattern in the sand. It showed you and I together to the end.'

'And after the end?'

'The pattern was not clear. Let me with you.'

Simon leaned across and kissed her very gently on the lips. 'You will always be with me, Guenara. Nothing shall part us after this game is played through to the ending.'

He shouted down for the others to remain there in case the Baron should slip past them and try to escape. If he did this, they were to kill him instantly.

The air in the loft was cool, a draught blowing through from somewhere up to their left. They crawled along, up and over the massive beams, through eons of dust. The wind grew fresher and a point of light appeared.

It was the edge of another door, left ajar. Simon pushed Guenara behind him and softly reached out to touch it. His nerves were strung taut anyway, and the sudden voice from the roof made him jump and bang his head on a rafter.

'Commander Rack. I have awaited your coming. Pray join me on the top of the world.'

Twister in one hand, sword in the other, Simon Rack walked out on to the roof of Castle Falcon, followed by Guenara. Baron Mescarl faced him ten paces away, and ten further paces was the edge of the roof. There were no battlements on that side, overlooking the precipice. He was dressed in the same black robes and cloak he had worn since the death of his cousin, the Lady Jocasta. The gold chain of the Mescarls hung about his neck and his slim sword was in his hand.

'So, Simon Rack. I would not have known you. A wretched wine-boy, a rebellious page, now returned to the planet of his birth to alter a millennium of history. De Poictiers suspected you from the start. I should have followed his wisdom and had you put down when you came stinking from the lair of the worm. And this woman. Who is she?'

'My name is Guenara. I was the woman of the wolfshead, Morkyn, slain by Simon Rack. Now I am his woman.'

The black beard tilted as he laughed, his chins quivering at the thought. 'So. Poor Magus. He promised me that not even a bear could topple Morkyn. Yet a lean wolf may do it. Eh? Now. What? Should I allow you to lead me in chains – the greatest lord of Sol Three? So that I may sweat out my time for an eternity on a stinking midden swinging round the far side of a dark tomorrow. And be "re-educated"! No! I think not. So it must end here. I see you have taken the step I feared. The forbidden weapons. Nothing could have been more strongly proscribed. Only an outworlder like you would have dared. You do not need it here, Simon. See, I throw my blade to the wind.'

Without even looking behind him, the Baron swung his sword away into the air, so that it hung for a moment like a living thing, then plunged into the abyss. The wind up there was strong enough for them to hear no sound of its falling. Gazing intently into that powerful face, Simon threw the gun down behind him, so that it lay near the door.

'Cautious, Commander!' chided Mescarl. 'I am tired of these games. I gambled and I had not thought one chance in a million weighed against me. Yet I was wrong. Now I and all my fellows must pay.'

'My lord, unless I am sadly wrong, you did not intend to carry through the game with your fellow players. Unless I am in error, there was another layer to your strategy.'

'What?'

'Another pheronium deposit. Bigger, perhaps? And to the north and not the south.'

Again the big man bayed his laughter to the world. 'If only you had stayed with me at the Castle Falcon! You would have made a shrewder adviser than my . . . No matter as to that. You will find it out in a day, so why should I not tell you? Aye, pheronium. Bigger! Huge deposits, great enough to run every star-ship in the Federation fleet for a hundred years. And there may be more. I would first have pushed up the price, then bought out every rival. They would not have dared stand against me. They were animals, Simon. Their dreams of power were petty things. They wished money and grander demesnes. I, I could have ruled the universe. Now you have taken it all from me. I have lost even my castle.'

Simon was not moved. 'You forfeited all right to sympathy, my lord, many years ago. You have degraded and debased men to a lower level than animals. As for your castle, it will no doubt stand, under Federation control. I will recommend they appoint a Protector to run it.'

'Who? Some low-bred lackey?'

Simon smiled. 'Hardly. I am minded to recommend my lord the Seneschal. I know no man who would run it better than de Poictiers. Old scores are useless; I have learnt that. I feel no great triumph for myself that I have brought you low. I have done my duty for my Service. I had thought I would remember my parents at this time.'

Mescarl looked puzzled. 'Your parents! Why on earth should you . . .? Of course. De Poictiers mentioned it to me, but it escaped my mind. He hanged your parents.'

'Yes. He hanged them because he knows no other rule in life than to obey authority as best he can. So he will make a fine Protector of Castle Falcon. Now we have talked enough. Will you come with me, or will I slay you?'

Guenara spoke for the first time. 'Can you not see, my lord? He has death writ clear across his brow. He will take his own life.' As she spoke, she had stepped nearer to the Baron, between him and Simon.

At that moment Mescarl pointed his heavy gauntlet

behind Simon to the Black Tower. 'See, the Armoury burns! It will soon rise to the skies, and take us all with it.'

Inevitably, Simon turned to look where the finger pointed. Faster than seemed possible for such a fat man, Mescarl used his moment.

From under his cloak, he produced a second sword and he leaped forward and lunged in one flickering movement.

Not at Simon.

At Guenara.

Her eye caught the glint of the sword and she turned to face it. The steel clashed through her half-open mouth, cutting her lips apart. Smashed and splintered teeth, tore through the back of her throat, nicked the spine and stood a hand's span out behind her neck.

There were no last words. For the death that she had seen in the sand, alone in the blackness of the forest, came too swiftly.

Her body fell against Simon, baulking his spring at Mescarl. The Baron left his sword where it lay and stepped back to the very edge of the roof.

'You took what I valued most. My castle and my plans. It seemed only fair that I should take something that you value. No tears, Simon? Save them. They do nobody a service. Now, before you jump at me waving your brand, I will leave you. Adieu, Simon. Enjoy your triumph.'

So saying, Richard de Guesclin Lawrence Mescarl, twenty-fourth and last legitimate Baron Mescarl, stepped quietly off the open roof of Castle Falcon and plunged to his death on the rocks beneath.

It was just before four o'clock in the afternoon of a warm day.

Simon did not walk over to see the body, how it lay. He dropped his bloody sword and sat down on the windswept roof and put his hand on the hair of Guenara.

And wept.

Epilogue
A Restless Farewell

'Perhaps it's better that way. Saves a lot of time and trouble. Shame about the woman. Eh?'

'Yes, sir.'

'Someone like her . . . could have used her in the Service. Still, there it is. Not a bad ending.' Colonel Stacey turned to look at Bogie. 'Ensign Bogart; I would be greatly obliged if you would do me a favour?'

'Of course, sir. Anything.'

'Stop picking at that revolting lump of flesh you insist on referring to as your nose! Thank you. Now, there seems to have been your usual quota of crass mistakes, but the end-result could have been worse. I'll reserve my final judgement until I read your written reports – which I'll expect on my desk by ten hundred tomorrow. You can dismiss until ten hundred the day after, when we'll finally debrief and I'll talk to you about a tricky little patrol problem that's come up in Sigma Nine. Right.'

Simon stood up to attention. Bogart stood up and coughed meaningfully behind his hand.

'Commander. Does this ill-shaped hunk of dreck have some sickening ailment he contracted on Sol Three, or is it merely a subtle device to draw my notice to something?'

Bogart came to attention. 'Sir, there's just . . . I think we have some leave coming to us.'

Stacey smiled – thinly. 'Now, let me see. I've got something on my desk here about leave for you two. You may be quite right, Ensign.' He rummaged through a pile of coloured folders in the right-hand tray, peering at the inscriptions coded into the sec-locks. Finally, he picked up a light green file.

'Wait a minute. Isn't this . . .? What an amazing thing, gentlemen. You remember that nasty business on Sturdal. A trader was supposed to have been killed by someone posing as a GalSec officer. Here's the folder about it.'

Simon and Bogart exchanged glances out of the corners of their eyes. Simon moved his fingers rapidly along the seam of his uniform trousers in the sign that meant 'Let's get out. Fast.'

'Stop wriggling, Commander! I haven't had a chance to look at this since you went to Sol Three. Perhaps I might get a chance to read it while you have your leave.'

Bogart coughed again. 'Permission to speak, sir. Perhaps my memory was at fault. I don't think there is any leave owing to us, sir. Not just now.'

The green file vanished back near the bottom of the pile.

'Right. Report here ten hundred tomorrow. Both of you back here at that time the next day. Dismiss.'

The two officers swung sharply to the salute and marched to the door. Bogart went through first, followed by Simon. They were actually in the corridor when Stacey called Simon back. Raising an eyebrow at Bogie, he wheeled about.

'What about this albino? Magus? What happened to him?'

Simon's jaw tightened. 'After Mescarl killed himself, we spent a long time trying to break into Magus's room. Finally, I had to use a grenade against the door. It's odd, because it only seemed to be an ordinary bronze alloy. It should have been easy to force. When we got in, we found the door had been locked on the inside. All the windows were heavily barred and locked. From the inside. I searched that chamber myself for hours, and I'd swear there was no hiding-place. No panels in the walls, floor or ceiling.'

'And?'

'The rooms were empty, sir. Magus had simply vanished.'